DEATH CALLS AT THE PALACE

A CHARLOTTE EDGERTON MYSTERY

Adele Fasick

MonganBooks

SAN FRANCISCO, CALIFORNIA

Book Layout ©2013 BookDesignTemplates.com

Cover design by Kit Foster Design.

Death Calls at the Palace/ Adele Fasick. -- 1st ed.
ISBN 978-0-9853152-5-2

I wander thro' each charter'd street
Near where the charter'd Thames does
flow.
And mark in every face I meet
Marks of weakness, marks of woe.

William Blake   "London"

CHAPTER ONE

A Bad Beginning

London, January1846

Charlotte woke to the sound of rain splattering on the window. Daniel was already up and stood at the wash basin peering into the tiny scrap of mirror on the wall as he tried to shave neatly. A gray light from the bare window showed the heavy bulk of a chest of drawers against the wall and two straight chairs in front of a dingy table.

"I should have been up before you and gone out for some bread," Charlotte muttered guiltily, not moving.

"You rest yourself. I have to be off to work, but I'll come back as early as I can and bring some food with me," her husband answered. He came over and sat on the bed next to her. "We've had a hard beginning to our life in London. I know how much you wanted to see your mother. We tried. Now there's nothing we can do."

"I can't bear it! I can't bear it!" The words felt as though they were torn out of her. Daniel took her in his arms and rocked her like a baby. Then with a final kiss, he reluctantly stood up.

"We'll get through this. We'll get through it together." He paused and looked around the desolate room. "But I have to leave you. I can't lose my job on top of everything else. Look, the rain is stopping. Go out and take a walk. Maybe the sun will come out. And I'll come back just as soon as I can." With that he was gone.

Charlotte couldn't force herself out of bed. She lay back, pulled the flimsy blanket up to her chin, and tried to will herself back to sleep. But all she could do was stare at the wet windows and watch them grow lighter. Finally she slowly lowered her feet to the floor and stood up. She would do as Daniel asked. She had no right to be a burden.

It was an effort to pull on her stockings and slip into her shoes. How the world had changed in only two days. When their ship had pulled into the London dock on Monday, Charlotte had half expected her mother would be there to greet her. She looked from face to face in the waiting crowd, but saw no one familiar. No one smiled at her or noticed her eager searching eyes. She and Daniel collected their things and made their way to the lodgings by themselves. Charlotte shivered as a cold rain started the minute they arrived at their lodgings.

At the house next door Daniel was able to pick up the key the landlady had left for them along with a letter addressed to Charlotte. The note was not from her mother, it was from a neighbor who wrote laboriously. *"I am sorry to write that your mother died of the fever several weeks ago. Your brother Tom asked me to send word to you. He went North with Betty to find work. Your mother was well buried. We all pray for you."* It was signed "Anne Taylor."

The awkward writing scrawled on a torn bit of paper reminded Charlotte that most of her neighbors could barely write their names. A message as long as this would be a chore for any of them. And her brother Tom probably never learned to write either. Young Tom— he had been only a child when Charlotte left. And times were bad. There would have been no school for him.

The memory of their dreary arrival swirled in her head as Charlotte pulled her faithful gray woolen shawl over her shoulders and walked onto the street. A pale sun was beginning to push through the milky clouds. The air was sharp, but not as cold as it had been in New York when they left. She bought a slice of bread and butter and a cup of coffee from a coffee stall and wandered down the street munching her bread and butter. She knew her genteel friends back in America would not have approved of eating on the street, but somehow in busy, grimy London it didn't seem to matter. No one would care whether she looked respectable or not. She felt invisible among the strangers around her.

As she walked toward Covent Garden, the streets became more crowded with men and women on their way to work and with the carts of barrow men selling everything from ham sandwiches to apples. The woman selling apples had a baby tied in a shawl around her body. The sight brought tears to Charlotte's eyes. The child looked so much like Brian, her own son who had died in October. She paused to buy an apple and gazed at the baby. "You have a handsome boy," she remarked to the young woman who only smiled shyly as she handed Charlotte an apple. Noting the interaction, the man at the next stall called out brusquely, "Hurry up, Polly, you don't have time to chat with customers."

Charlotte's mind was on her own child. Brian's death was what had driven Daniel to take the position on the London newspaper, so Charlotte could visit her mother and get over her grief. Her mother had lost several babies as infants. She would understand Charlotte's feelings of emptiness. Everyone lost young children; babies are fragile creatures. But Charlotte hadn't realized how deeply the loss would eat into her heart after only four months of love and dreams crammed into Brian's young life. Her mother would understand, but now her mother was gone.

As she walked further and further away from Cecil Court where they were lodging, Charlotte could hear shouts coming from a crowd ahead. She hurried toward the sound, glad to get away from the circling thoughts of grief. When she entered Golden Square, the crowd was suddenly in front of her. Most of the men were dressed in working clothes. Painters with their paper hats and bakers still wearing their flour- smeared aprons rubbed shoulders with burly laborers. Scores of men, some holding placards reading "A vote for every man" or "Support the Charter" milled around the square, while on a small platform in the center a man struggled to make himself heard.

Several women were scattered through the crowd and Charlotte pushed her way forward so she could get closer to the platform. She wanted to hear what the speaker was saying. Perhaps Daniel would need to know the story. A dozen or so policemen patrolling the edges of the crowd looked nervous as they surveyed the growing numbers of demonstrators entering the square from surrounding streets. Suddenly one of the demonstrators whirled around and shouted something at one of the policemen. Charlotte couldn't hear what was said but she saw the policeman raise his truncheon and strike out. Men on both sides of the policeman started shouting and soon there was a melee that spread across the square.

Charlotte turned to leave, but found her way blocked by a moving tide of men and women advancing toward the center of the square. Behind her she could hear a crash as though someone had thrown a stone through a window. Charlotte shoved her way through the dense crowd toward the side of the square to find a way out. Any street would do if she could only get out of the frightening crowd. She pushed a woman who was blocking her path and regretted it when the woman screamed at her, "Sure are you such a lady you can't fight back? Kill the bullies!"

Panting and clutching her shawl around her shoulders, Charlotte fought her way to a side street and slipped out of the square into a sudden quiet. She paused to readjust her shawl and smooth her hair and then walked away from the crowd as quickly as she could. The houses were bigger now and the street was empty except for two servant girls clutching packages and a few footmen standing outside the house doors looking longingly at the excitement down at the square.

The street ahead meandered toward a square, but none of it looked familiar to Charlotte. She turned to look back the way she had come, but the fighting was still going on and she knew she couldn't go back that way. As she stood looking up and down the street, she noticed a man dressed in an elegant morning suit walking toward her. He might have been a prosperous businessman except for his dark complexion and his long black beard. Instead of a top hat he was wearing a blue turban on his head. When he got close to her, he paused and asked, "Can I help you in any way, madam? Have you been injured by those ruffians in the square?"

"I am quite unhurt. The disturbance in the square simply makes my path back to my home more difficult. I am trying to find the best way to walk back to Cecil Court."

"Will you permit me to accompany you for a short distance to show you the way?" the Indian man asked politely. "London streets can be confusing to people who are new to the city. Please allow me to introduce myself. My name is Kumar Singh, I live near-by and I know where Cecil Court is."

"I will be grateful if you can show me the way," Charlotte replied. "My husband and I arrived in London this week and I am not familiar with the city streets."

Kumar Singh bowed in acknowledgement and the two of them set off down the street away from the still noisy square. Charlotte could feel the eyes of the peddlers on her as she walked with the Indian man. She searched her mind to find something suitable to say, but aside from a banal remark upon the improving weather, could find nothing. The two of them walked in companionable silence for a few minutes until they reached a crossing that looked familiar to Charlotte.

"Oh, here we are," she exclaimed. "We are right back in Cecil Court. That brick house with the green door is where my husband and I are lodging. My husband, Daniel Gallagher, is an editor with the *London Weekly Newspaper*. I am sure he will be glad to hear that I have found such friendly help in a new city. Thank you very much, Mr. Singh."

"You are most welcome, madam. I hope that I will be able to be of service again in the future."

Charlotte made her way quickly into the house, glad to be out of the noise and confusion of the city streets. The little sitting room that had looked so grim in the morning was brightened a bit as the afternoon sun crept in through the window. Perhaps she could make this meager lodging into a comfortable home after all.

CHAPTER TWO

Meetings and News

During the afternoon a light rain started and when Daniel came home, he was carrying two baked potatoes bought from a barrow man on the street. "Here's some good hot food to keep the chill away," he said as he came in. "I wrapped them in my scarf so they are still hot."

Charlotte set some plates on the table in the small front parlor on the first floor. As she ate, Charlotte realized how hungry she had been, although it had been days since she had thought about meals. The buttery potatoes tasted better than anything she had eaten since they arrived in London.

"Oh Daniel, I still haven't gone down to the basement to try out the stove and see what kind of pots and pans we will need. I'm not used to a house like this, so tall and narrow with the kitchen in the basement. But I will start cooking decent meals soon. I promise. I don't know what has gotten into me since we arrived. I haven't been able to shake off my gloom, but now I'm feeling a little better. Today I had quite an adventure. You won't believe what happened when I walked over to Charing Cross. The crowds were awful and people starting hurling things at the police…"

She was interrupted by a steady knocking at the door. Daniel went to see who was there and came back to the parlor with a slight young woman wearing a dark gray skirt and clutching a plaid shawl around her shoulders. Charlotte did not recognize her, but the woman spoke up quickly.

"You are Charlotte Edgerton, my Tom's sister, aren't you? I don't suppose you remember me. I was only a child when you went away. Betty Baker I was although my father was no baker. And now I am Betty Edgerton and your sister." She paused for breath.

Charlotte was overwhelmed by the flow of words coming from the pale young woman—hardly more than a girl—who clutched her shawl closely around her and looked anxiously around the room. She answered quickly to reassure her.

"Oh you are Betty! I know Tom got married. My mother wrote to us with the news. Did she not show you the letter I wrote offering you and Tom our best wishes?"

"It would have done no good if she had," answered Betty. "I never learned to read. Nor did Tom. There's no one in your family got as much learning as you did. And your mother was feeling poorly for all of last year before she died. God rest her soul! She may have forgotten to read your letter to us. We have been all in a tumble since then. Tom was terribly upset. I had never seen him cry before, but we all cried at your mother's funeral."

"Where is Tom?" Charlotte asked. "Is he with you?"

"No, it's terrible bad news I have about Tom," Betty answered. "I don't know what to do."

"What happened?" Daniel asked quickly.

"Tom and I went to hear the speeches at that meeting in Charing Cross today. But there was a lot of trouble. The police started fighting with the men carrying cards. I don't know what they were saying or what they were so angry about. First thing you know they were all fighting and Tom was pulling me away to the side to keep me safe. But then a policeman fell and his head started bleeding. Most of the demonstrators ran off, Tom and me just stood there a minute not knowing what to do. Then a policeman grabbed Tom and said he was taking him to prison—assaulting a policeman he said, but Tom didn't do anything."

Charlotte's throat tightened with fear. "Where did they take him? And how did you get away?"

"The policemen didn't want me. They took Tom and some of the other men. 'You run', Tom told me. 'You find Charlotte in Cecil Court'. So here is where I've come and I did find you, didn't I?"

"I'm glad you remembered the address we sent in that letter even if you couldn't read it, Betty."

The three of them went downstairs to the gloomy kitchen and made a fire in the old wood stove.

Charlotte was able to boil water for tea and they sat down at the long wooden table to talk about what could be done. Betty and Tom had no place to stay in London. They had walked there all the way from Bristol, sleeping overnight in farmers' barns when Tom could do chores to earn them a meal and shelter. The last two nights they had spent huddled in the doorway of a church in London. Charlotte insisted Betty should stay with them for a few days until they could find out what the police would do about Tom.

Daniel walked over to the police court to see whether he could get any news of what had happened to Tom and the other demonstrators that had been picked up. He found a crowd of friends and relatives milling around the doorway, but they were all sent home by a gruff policeman who yelled. "Nothing tonight. The judge will be here in the morning. Go home! Go home! Or I'll bring you all in."

After a restless night Charlotte and Betty walked to the police court early in the morning. There were no seats left, so they joined the throng of women and children crowding around the door to see what was happening to the men. They couldn't see much. At a large table at the front of the room sat a solemn looking man who must have been the magistrate. He seemed to be giving a speech, but neither Charlotte nor Betty could hear what he said. One by one the men who had been detained after the demonstration were brought before him. There were some questions asked, answers mumbled, a paper signed, and then each man was let go, usually to be met by squeals and cries of joy from the family waiting for him.

As the minutes crept by and turned into an hour, Charlotte worried that Tom would never appear. Finally Betty clutched her arm and cried, "It's him. It's my Tom!" and pointed to one of the prisoners stepping up to the table. They saw Tom bend over the table to write something and then he turned to leave.

Soon the three of them were out on the street. Charlotte looked at her tall, red-headed brother and could barely see the child she remembered in the face of this young man who stood in front of her. He was unshaven and his shirt was torn, but his smile was bright as he hugged Betty and held her close.

"Why Tom, I never would have known you if I had met you on the street."

"I would have known you, sister Charlotte, you look just as you used to but more like a teacher than ever. I'll expect to see you wearing spectacles soon. And what do you think of my blooming Betty? Would you believe she was the little Betty Baker who used to tag after you when we played games?"

Betty said nothing but hung onto Tom's arm as though she would never let go.

"Why did they let everyone leave?" asked Charlotte. "I don't know why the men were arrested yesterday nor why they were released so fast. What happened?"

"A couple of the policemen were battered a bit, but no one was hurt bad. And there's no place to keep prisoners for very long. The police certainly don't want to feed them, so they had to let us go. Except they asked everyone if he was a foreigner, because they said they would send foreigners back to where they came from. I guess Bristol wasn't far enough away to be foreign." He laughed at the thought.

"What was it you had to sign?"

"The magistrate said it was a promise not to disrupt the Queen's peace and not to get into trouble again. I wrote my 'X' and they let me go."

The rest of the day was busy. After cleaning up and getting something to eat, Tom went off to find work. Charlotte and Betty went to the market to buy pans and utensils to make the kitchen useable again, and some food to cook at home. By the time Daniel came home from the newspaper office, the women had a fish stew bubbling on the stove and potatoes roasting in the oven. The three of them shared the first meal Charlotte served in their new home.

Tom didn't get back until almost 10 o'clock that night. He had found work unloading cargo from a barge on the Thames, so he brought a few pence with him and a pint of beer to share.

"There was lots of talk down on the docks about the trouble at Charing Cross. It was the Chartists, they said, who were protesting. When my mates heard I was there, they wanted to know all about how many police were hurt and whether any of the demonstrators had been kept in jail."

"Were they glad to hear that most of the demonstrators were honest workmen and had no thought of hurting anyone?" asked Betty.

"Oh, not so glad. I never heard such wild talk as I heard from the men on the dock. 'Too bad they were fighting police instead of going after the Queen' one of them said. That's what he said."

Betty was pale with shock. "I never knew people would try to kill the Queen. And her such a pretty young woman too. London is too much for me. There's too many wicked things going on here."

"There's many who would kill the Queen, and her foreign husband too." Tom insisted. "You should hear the men talking in the pub where I stopped. They said the same. It's a republic they want—just like America. That's what they say."

CHAPTER THREE

Learning Their Letters

Tom found work on the quays almost every day and earned money to pay for food, although there was seldom enough left over to pay a bit of rent for their lodging. Betty was determined to bring in money to help with expenses. Growing up in the country she had learned a lot about plants and she had a cheerful, friendly smile, so she was soon able to persuade one of the barrow women who sold flowers in the streets around Covent Gardens to let her help. Every day she went to the busy market to trim dead leaves and keep the flowers looking fresh. She could sell flowers to even the grumpiest housewife or passer-by. Every day she earned a few pennies to add to Tom's wages, but she still found much of life in London confusing.

"There's signs everywhere and people bring me notes with the names of flowers on them. So many people here know how to read. I've got to learn real quick," she declared. "It's bad enough in the country when I can't read signs or write a letter, but in the city Tom and me will never last if we can't read. There's so much writing going on in a place like this that it's frightening.. Will you teach me to read, Charlotte? Tom told me you was a teacher and I'll work real hard, I promise. "

After that, almost every afternoon when Betty returned from work, she and Charlotte sat down in the kitchen to work at the long table. Although the kitchen was below ground level, two windows, high on the wall, let in light from the area in front of the house, a small unpaved space where a bare scrawny tree hung over the pump, the source of all of their water. Patiently Charlotte went over the letters while Betty copied them and learned their names

A for apple

B for butter ("and for Betty" she added)

C for cow

Betty copied the letters on spoiled sheets of paper Daniel brought home from the newspaper office. The day that she was able to write "Betty Edgerton" and show it to Tom was a proud one for her. Tom himself wanted to learn to read, but he had to leave early in the morning to be on the docks when the ships came in and needed unloading. The men who were there early were chosen for work. By the time he got home at night it was 9 or 10 o'clock and when he looked at the letters the women were writing, his head slumped over and he fell asleep at the table.

"I have a clever wife who can write her own name and mine too. I don't need to learn to write myself," he claimed.

Even without Tom, Charlotte's class was growing. Betty was enthusiastic and talked about her lessons with everyone she met at the market. Soon she asked Charlotte if it would be all right for her friend Deirdre to share the sessions with her. Then Deirdre brought her younger sister, Kathleen, who had recently come from Ireland because of the hard times there. They shifted the class time to the evening after the women finished their work. Deirdre was a scullery maid in a house near Charing Cross, and Kathleen worked as a laundress.

Charlotte had never taught grown women before and she wasn't sure whether they would like the simple rhymes she used with the primary children in America. They started out just learning the letters. Charlotte watched while Deirdre struggled to make the curve in the letter 'D'.

"It must be hard to come and work so hard after your day's work," she said to the young woman. "What is it that makes you so eager to learn to read and write?"

"It's the thought of my mother still back in Ireland and with the children to take care of. Sure, she must be lonely day after day with no word from us. And it's precious little money we've been able to send. If I could write a letter and tell her that we are working hard and saving money, it would make her so happy. It's easy to find a neighbor who could read the letter to her."

Charlotte could understand that feeling easily enough. Daniel had struggled through his first years in Boston trying desperately to save enough money to send for his mother and sister. But they were lucky enough to be able to write to one another occasionally. Sending a letter was expensive, but it wasn't completely out of reach now that it was possible for the sender to pay in advance so the person who received the letter was not charged for delivery. That gave Charlotte an idea for how she could teach the girls to write. She made up a series of sentences:

I am thinking of you, Mother.

How are Neal and Martin?

Kathleen and I have good food to eat every night.

We have found an English friend named Betty.

Our teacher's name is Mrs. Gallagher.

Those sentences meant a lot to Deirdre and Kathleen and they copied them enthusiastically at every opportunity. Soon they started looking at the books Charlotte showed them and deciphering the letters. One evening when she came in for her lesson, Deirdre had an adventure to tell.

"I was sitting out in the little yard outside the kitchen. Peeling potatoes I was. And I stopped for just a minute to study a bit of that story in the book you lent me. The cook came out of the kitchen and started screeching at me, but you'll not believe what happened then.

"The master himself came to the kitchen door to see what was going on. I'd not seen him before because it was the cook who took me on for kitchen help. He's a man like none I've ever seen. He looks like one of the wise men in the Christmas pageant we saw last year. He has a long black beard and one of those scarves wrapped around his head instead of a hat. Blue it was, a beautiful blue like the sky in Ireland. And he was kind as can be. 'Let the child read if she has finished her work', he said to the cook. 'Reading is a good thing. And I'll not have yelling in my household'."

"I know that man," Charlotte said. "That must be Mr. Singh, who helped me find my way home on the day of the big demonstration. I never knew you worked in his kitchen. He seemed like a very pleasant gentleman and I'm glad he helped you."

"Why does he have such a long beard and why does he wear that strange blue scarf?"

"It's his religion," explained Charlotte. "He comes from India, I think, and they have different religions there and different ways of dressing."

"You mean he is a heathen? The priest told us there were people like that. People who don't know about Jesus or the saints. I've never seen a heathen before."

Betty and Kathleen were watching this conversation with wide eyes. "I've never seen a heathen either," admitted Betty. "I don't think we had any heathen in Bristol. Are they Americans?"

"Mr. Singh comes from India. That is different from America. A lot of English soldiers are fighting in India now because there has been a rebellion against the Queen. We will have to read some more newspapers to find out more about it."

Charlotte sighed as she and Betty tidied up the kitchen table putting away the papers they had been practicing with. There was a long way to go and a lot of reading to do before the young women learned enough about the world to understand London and their new life in the city.

CHAPTER FOUR

An Unexpected Meeting

On Saturday afternoon, after Daniel's work was done, he and Charlotte went for a walk to explore more of the city. They had not gone far when Charlotte saw a familiar figure ahead of her. It was Kumar Singh. His pale blue turban bobbed above heads of other pedestrians as he walked. Charlotte pointed him out to Daniel.

"I seldom see a man so tall," Daniel commented. "His carriage makes me think he must be an army man. I wonder what he is doing in London."

Kumar Singh was walking toward them, and as he approached he recognized Charlotte and bowed slightly toward her. Daniel seized the opportunity to speak to him.

"I have not met you, sir, but my wife tells me that you kindly directed her when she was bewildered by the crowd at the Chartist demonstration. I want to thank you for your kindness. We are strangers in London and have not learned our way about the city very well."

"It was my pleasure to assist the lady," the Sikh answered politely. "I trust that no harm came to either of you."

"Oh no," Charlotte interjected. "The crowd that day was not ferocious. I do not know how the trouble started, but I would like to learn more. "

"Yes, as a newspaper man I am trying to learn all that I can about the disturbances in the city. If you saw how the disturbance started, I would like very much to talk with you further about it," Daniel added.

A smile came to Singh's face as he heard what Daniel said. "Ah, a journalist! I am eager to talk to a newspaperman.   I will be very glad to tell you all I can about the demonstration last week and perhaps you would be interested in hearing more about the purpose of my visit to this country. My wife and I have met very few English people here."

Neither Daniel nor Charlotte could resist the chance to learn more about this exotic stranger in their midst. Charlotte quickly invited him to call on them soon. "Sunday afternoon is a good time for us to receive visitors," she said. "We would be very happy to see you and your wife."

On the following Sunday afternoon Charlotte was reading the new issue of the *London Weekly Newspaper*, while Daniel was working at his desk when they were startled by a loud rap on the door. Kumar Singh was standing on the doorstep, rain glistening on his umbrella. Next to him stood a small woman bundled up in a dark shawl that covered most of her body. Daniel quickly invited them in and as they took off their wet outer garments, Charlotte saw that the woman was dressed in a long, tunic with a pattern of red and yellow flowers, and wide-legged blue trousers. Her hair was hidden by a high turban decorated by a chain of gold and she wore a flowing silk scarf covering her shoulders.

"This is my wife, Meena Kaur," Kumar Singh told them. "We hope this is a good time to call on you."

The young woman pressed her two hands together, bowed her head slightly and murmured a few words in a foreign language. She selected a chair close to her husband and sat down quietly. Charlotte wondered whether she spoke any English but did not want to ask.

Charlotte and Daniel welcomed the couple and then Charlotte went downstairs to make tea. By the time she carried the tray upstairs, the two men were deep in conversation. When she came in, Kumar Singh was talking about the demonstration.

"I saw something of what happened that day. There was a speaker's platform at the front of the crowd upon which several men were sitting. I saw Feargus O'Connor, the fiery Irish political leader, among them, but I did not hear him speak. Another man was making a speech. He was somewhat disheveled looking and with a strange accent, although he looked English enough."

"I believe he was probably one of the miners from Lancashire," Daniel interjected. "Could you understand what he was saying?"

"Yes, he was urging the crowd to march to the Palace and give their petition to the Queen 'We must speak directly to the throne' he shouted. Then he led the protesters in a song. Some of the men sang along. They sang it several times and I remember some of it. :

Ye working men of Britain come listen awhile,
Concerning the cotton spinners who lately stood their trial
Transported for seven years far, far awa'

Several of the men around me started walking in the direction of the Palace. They were strong looking working men and the scene was a rather frightening one.

"A group of four or five policemen drew up before the men who were walking and tried to hold them back. The police did not want them to leave the square and go toward the Palace. That was when the shouting grew louder and someone threw a brick at the police. It was a brawl, but at first the police and the demonstrators seemed evenly matched.

"Mr. O'Connor stood up on the platform and urged his followers to be peaceful. 'There will be no violence against the crown' he shouted. Many people listened to him and calmed down but others only became angrier. I hoped the crowd would disperse peacefully, but I did not want to be involved in fighting if they did not, so I turned to leave. When I looked back I saw that one of the policemen had fallen."

"That must have been shortly before you met me and showed me the way to Cecil Court," Charlotte added.

"Yes indeed. I did not want to remain in the area when people were fighting or when they were shouting about going to the Palace. I myself wish to go to the Palace and win an audience with the Queen, but I do not want to act like those young workmen men did. And I do not expect to be treated the way they were treated. I am a representative of my fellow Sikhs and I expect to be treated with respect. As I started to leave and saw you, Mrs. Gallagher, alone on the street, I felt that I had to offer assistance."

"We are grateful for your help," Daniel said, "My newspaper wrote an account of the demonstration and the arrests. Perhaps you read the article in the *London Weekly Illustrated*. But we could not find any men who admitted being there and were willing to talk to a newspaper. You say you saw the young policeman fall. Do you remember seeing anyone in the crowd throwing a rock? Or carrying one? There were other policemen about. What did they see? Did no one see the attacker? Why was he not detained?"

Charlotte was not surprised that Kumar Singh did not answer immediately and she spoke up. "I was at the demonstration too, you know, and I remember the confusion and the crowd. I was not close enough to the platform to see the attack, but I would not be surprised to hear that no one noticed the man who hit the policeman."

"That is true, I am trying to remember people I saw near the speaker, but I am afraid my eyes were directed toward the fallen policeman." Kumar Singh seemed eager to move on to other topics. "I am sure that you are wondering what I am doing in London. You may know from my turban that I am a Sikh who traveled here from India. I have known many Englishmen, although I have seldom had the pleasure of talking with an English woman. In my country women do not often appear in public. Indeed my wife has seldom left the house where we are staying."

He glanced toward his wife, who remained silent, and then continued talking. "My father was an officer who served the Maharajah Rajit Singh. We have received representatives from the East Indian Company for many years and I was given a good English education as well as studying traditional texts with my guru. Alas my father died several years ago and since then the British have been disrespectful in many ways. They have treated us as enemies, people to be ruled instead of comrades and allies. Sikhs are a proud people. We do not need the British to rule over us although we are quite willing to do business with them and to trade with them."

"What brings you to London then, if you have suffered such poor treatment?" Daniel wanted to know.

"I have met several Englishmen that I respect and admire. One of them became a friend and a hunting companion of mine. He persuaded me that the rulers of the country, the Queen and her husband, were enlightened rulers who wanted to have friendly relations with people living in their colonies. He once told me that she would listen to the concerns of all of her people."

"Have you been able to have an audience with the Queen?" asked Charlotte, awed by the idea of anyone who might achieve that.

Kumar Singh was clearly disturbed by the question. "Unfortunately I have been unable to obtain the audience I had hoped for," he admitted. "I have presented myself several times and have explained that I wish to deal directly with the British government. But each time I am told that I must speak to someone from the East India Company. Those are the very people who have been mistreating our people, especially in the Punjab. One of them stole a treasure from my family. It is the officials of that company about whom I wish to complain. "

"Is no one willing to speak to you?"

"I recently received a letter from one gentleman who has suggested a meeting. He is someone I met briefly in India when he was stationed in the Punjab. He is Captain Hugh Granville. Perhaps you know the name?"

"I have not heard of the man," Daniel replied, while Charlotte just shook her head. "Is he in the Army or does he work for the East India Company?"

"He has been a soldier in the 3rd Light Dragoons and served in India and Afghanistan so he is familiar with the situation there. I am not sure of his official position. He indicated that he has some influence in the Company and has contacts within government circles, but I have been unable to find out whether he is a man of influence." Singh frowned as he spoke.

"Do you think the British government knows how the East India Company has been behaving in your country?"

"I am sure they must. After all the Company has the full support of the British Army. Whenever anyone questions their actions, they find it easy enough to call in British troops. I myself have seen the troops arrest and imprison Indians who dared to protest against the Company. If the British crown is using this Company to do their work, they surely must take responsibility for the company's actions. As an Englishman yourself, do you not believe that your government controls its representatives abroad?"

Daniel nodded in agreement as Kumar continued. "My most serious complaint is that someone serving in the British Army or working within the company has committed an offense against my family and the honor of our religion. I have been holding this secret in my heart—the offense that was committed—but I will not be silent forever. If the British crown is not willing to punish those who bring disgrace on their country, I am afraid there will be more rebellion and fighting in the Punjab."

Daniel agreed with him. "My wife and I are both aware that the British government has encouraged British companies to increase their trade in many countries. And, of course, British companies are not always welcomed. There has been trouble in China as well as in India."

"As a woman who has lived these past five years in a country that rebelled against British rule," Charlotte added, "I can certainly sympathize with your people who do not want to yield to the English. I hope the problems can be worked out without causing violence."

"Ah, it is difficult to make changes in a government without using force. I am not a violent man, but I grew up in India, and I have learned that power is usually won by fighting. You British seem to think you can change things just by talking, but if people are unwilling to talk, what happens then?"

During all this conversation, Kumar Singh's wife said nothing. She leaned forward in her chair watching her husband talk, but Charlotte wondered how well she understood English. Could she follow what they were saying? She turned toward the woman.

"And what do you think, Mrs. Singh? Do you believe the English can change their ways and treat their colonies better?"

"Please, there is no need to call me Mrs. Singh. We Sikh women do not take our husband's name when we marry as you Europeans do. The British government has demanded that we start following that practice but I prefer our own tradition. My name is Meena Kaur and I hope you will call me Meena." Her voice was quiet, but she spoke English fluently and without hesitation.

"I am learning something new every day," Charlotte answered. "I like the idea of letting married women keep their own names. It is difficult to give up a name that has been yours for all of your life before marriage. So, please call me Charlotte. Then we can be real friends."

"My husband knows far more than I do about running the country," Meena continued, "but the English have not been listening to him. And yet the ruler of England is a woman. I do not understand how a woman could refuse to listen to a man as respected as my husband."

"You are a representative of your government, are you not?" asked Daniel.

Kumar frowned at the question. "The British government does not recognize the Sikhs as being a government. Our respected leader Ranjet Singh had power enough to influence the British, but he is dead. I am not an official diplomat and indeed I do not think that the British East India Company believes that any Indian could serve as a diplomat. But my people have ruled the Punjab for centuries and Sikhs are known as honorable people. We are willing to work with the British and trade with them, but we will not be insulted and dishonored by their Army or by this East India Company of theirs."

"And you say your family been insulted?"

"Last year my father gave a great banquet for a director of the Company, some of his associates, and a few Army officers. They were invited into our home. We shared a meal with them, gave each of them a proper gift and showed them our treasures. Our greatest treasure, one that was given to my father from his father and so for generations past is a Khanda, the sacred symbol of the Sikhs. The Khanda that has been in my family for many generations was carved from a large emerald. The royal jewel is a proper medium for such a sacred symbol. Alas, I believe some of our guests did not understand the symbol and one man who saw the traditional sword in the design said. 'Ah, your swords did not protect you from the British army, did they?' He laughed as he said it."

"Oh, that is insulting," Charlotte said. "Your father must have been bitterly wounded by such a remark."

"Thank you for your understanding, Mrs. Gallagher, but that was not the end of it. After our guests had left and the servants had cleared away the remains of the feast, we discovered that our precious Khanda had disappeared. Someone in the visiting group must have stolen it. What kind of man would steal a religious icon from his host? Such behavior is surely not tolerated in any civilized society. And yet, when I complained to the director of the Company, he suggested that one of my own servants must have stolen the jewel. No Sikh would ever do such a thing. It is incomprehensible to me that the Queen and the British government would allow a company that represents them to behave in this way."

"Has no one ever given you satisfaction about how such a theft could occur? Did your father speak to the Army about this?"

"Unfortunately, my father was not well even when he gave the dinner. After that evening and the shock of losing our family treasure, his heart gave way and he died suddenly. It is now my responsibility to find our Khanda and to see that it is returned to its place of honor."

"Perhaps, Mr. Singh, you will allow me to write a story for my newspaper about the Sikhs and their traditions. I do not know whether you would want me to refer to your personal loss, but many people in this country might be interested in hearing more about your country. Most English people know very little about the different provinces of India and the people who live there. Perhaps I could discuss with you the information that should be included."

"Ah, indeed sir. I should be honored to work with you on such a paper. That might be one way of calling the attention of the Queen, or perhaps Prince Albert, to the events in India. We are proud people and no individuals or company should dare to dishonor us." Kumar Singh clenched his fists and looked grim.

Daniel and Kumar Singh agreed to meet again in a few days to talk about Daniel's article. They were eager to start working on it, but Charlotte wondered whether the Queen would pay any attention to Daniel's article or to Kumar Singh.

CHAPTER FIVE

Police at the Door

A few days later when Charlotte was preparing a meal for Tom, who usually worked until nine or ten o'clock at night, she was startled by the sudden slamming of the front door. Charlotte looked up from the stove to see Tom standing at the kitchen door. He ran his fingers through his red hair and scowled as he burst into speech.

"There's more trouble at the Palace," he exclaimed. "As I was walking home from the quays, I heard shouting and people running. Someone has tried to kill the Queen or perhaps Prince Albert. Anyway, tonight one of the policemen guarding the Palace was shot dead and there are police and soldiers searching all over for the killer."

"Did anyone see who fired the shots?" Betty asked.

"No. Nobody saw who did it. The police are going to be looking for anyone they can blame for the crime. Maybe they'll pick on me because they already accused me once of something I did not do."

"No, Tom, that will never happen," Daniel reassured him. "They will be looking for people who were seen around the Palace earlier this evening. You weren't anywhere near there, were you?"

"Well, to tell you the truth, I did stop for a glass of ale at one of the pubs near the palace. I was passing it on the way back here and I was so tired I thought I deserved a bit of a drink to warm me. What if the police saw me there?"

The four of them talked into the night. Daniel and Charlotte tried to persuade Tom he was in no danger of being picked up for a crime. He seemed to accept their arguments and agreed the police were unlikely to single him out for questioning. By the time they all went to bed, Charlotte felt that his fears had been allayed and both Tom and Betty were calm.

Nonetheless, despite the reassurances she had given Tom and Betty, Charlotte passed a restless night. There was a lingering fear in her mind that perhaps Tom could be in some kind of danger. When she woke up, the morning was still dark and it seemed as if daylight would never come. The long, gray London mornings always made her feel mournful. Then came a knock on the bedroom door.

Betty stood in the doorway crying, "Tom went away during the night. He just ran off. I think he's afraid of the police. How will I ever find him?"

Betty's cry jolted Charlotte awake. At first she thought Tom might have gone out to get an early start on finding work, but she remembered how fearful he had been the night before. Perhaps he hadn't been as reassured as she had hoped. Did he still expect the police to come pursuing him?

When she gave Daniel his tea, she asked his opinion. "Tom had nothing to do with the shots fired yesterday. Can you believe the police would be looking for him? Why would they pick on him?"

"He was in trouble over the violence at the Chartist demonstration not long ago. Perhaps they remember him and think he is a troublemaker. I'll see what I can find out at the newspaper office or in the coffee shops around Covent Garden. Men there are always talking about politics and crime."

Betty dragged into the kitchen tying her apron strings with clumsy hands. Her hair had not been combed and her eyes were red with crying. "What will they do with my Tom?" she wailed. "How will I ever find him? Will they put him in prison?"

"They won't put him in prison," Daniel promised. "Somehow we will find him and let him know he's not in danger. But first we must find out where he is. I have to go to work now, but I will try to learn as much as I can about what the police are doing."

It took another hour for Charlotte to persuade Betty that the best thing for her to do would be to go to work as usual. The barrow woman was counting on her to help sell her wares. And Betty had recently started working as a laundress after the flower market closed in the morning. Between the two jobs, she could bring in almost as much money as Tom did. Knowing how important her work was, Betty reluctantly got dressed and left the house.

"Will you still be teaching my friends and me tonight?" Betty asked as she left. "I'm not sure I'll be able to learn anything what with all my worry about Tom, but I must learn to write so I can post notices and tell him to come back to us."

"That's a good idea," Charlotte agreed. "Tom can't have gone very far. He would never leave you for long, Betty. When he realizes he doesn't have to be afraid, he will come back I'm sure. Then we can decide what has to be done. Besides while you are out on the streets with the barrow woman, you may hear more news about what the police are doing."

Charlotte was left alone at last. She had to go to the market to buy food for their evening meal, but perhaps that would give her a chance to ask questions about the shooting. Surely everyone at the market would be talking about the death of the unfortunate policeman.

Before she could put on her bonnet and leave the house, she heard a loud banging at the door. When she opened it, two policemen were standing outside.

"Does Thomas Edgerton live here?" asked one of them.

"He has been staying with us for a while," Charlotte admitted slowly, "but he has left now. Why are you looking for him?"

"There has been a shooting at the palace and we are going to question all the radicals and disturbers of the peace in the city. If this Thomas Edgerton is here, you had better tell us," was the harsh answer.

"Mr. Edgerton is my brother and he is neither a radical nor a disturber of the peace. What makes you think that he is?"

"He attended the Chartist demonstration a few weeks ago and was involved in the disturbances against the police there. We are checking on all of the men picked up that night in for questioning. The citizens of London will not allow riot and rebellion here. We are not in France. We are law-abiding English people."

The other policeman who had been watching quietly broke in. "Are you going to help us find this brother of yours? The magistrate may be questioning everyone who has been involved in helping radicals and Chartists."

By the time the police left, Charlotte's face was flushed with anger. She closed the door with a bang. What was it she had heard her father quote? "An Englishman's home is his castle." It was no castle apparently if the police wanted to track someone down. She wondered whether the police would come into the house and search for Tom if they wanted so much to find him. When she finally made her way to the market, she was determined to ask everyone she met what they knew about the death of the policeman.

While Charlotte picked over the vegetables at the market, Daniel walked to a tavern close to the Palace where the shooting had taken place. He questioned the waiters and men who were clustered around the tavern and in the streets. He was determined to discover more about the mysterious death of the young policeman. No one could tell him much. The dead man's name was Sean Costello; he came from Bath and had been working as a policeman for more than a year. The bullet that struck him had been fired from a delivery wagon that was approaching the Palace from the front. As it approached, several guards had waved at the driver and gestured for him to go around to the rear entrance where deliveries were made. When the driver continued heading straight toward the Palace, Costello had approached the wagon.

That was when a single revolver shot was fired, not by the driver, but by someone who must have been hidden behind the mounds of fresh laundry in the open truck. Once the shot was fired and the policeman fell, the driver whipped up his animal and drove toward the gate. Other policemen and guards ran after the cart and the driver turned recklessly, crashing the wagon into the stone wall in front of the Palace.

The driver jumped out but was quickly detained by the guards. Spectators on the Palace grounds rushed over to right the wagon as bales of laundry cascaded from the overturned wagon and spilled onto the Palace grounds. In the confusion of picking up the laundry and trying to search the wagon, whoever had fired the shot disappeared. The driver claimed he knew nothing about the man who had hidden himself under the stacks of laundry in the cart. Several servants supported his story that he was a well-known tradesman who had been driving the cart of laundry to the Palace every week. The police finally let him go with a warning to be more careful about approaching the Palace.

Police and soldiers searched through the crowd asking whether anyone had seen a man with a revolver. They went through the loads on wagons and barrows and opened the packs of peddlers, but found no gun and no sign of bullets or of another weapon.

After he had gathered all the information he could, Daniel made his way to the newspaper office and sat at a desk to scribble notes for his story. A few minutes later the owner of the newspaper, George Reynolds, strode into the office.

"It has been a busy morning, Gallagher. I am afraid our paper may be in trouble. Perhaps we had better go to a coffee shop where we can discuss the sudden violence."

After the two of them walked to a nearby coffee house and settled into a quiet corner, Mr. Reynolds leaned across the table and spoke, "There is a great stir about town after this latest trouble, I'm sure you know that. Our paper will be cast as a villain by some people in this city. We have supported the rights of working men and written about the poverty in which most people are living these days. Aristocrats are forever predicting that writing such as ours will bring on violence and perhaps a revolution. There are many influential people in this city who do not like anyone to question the value of the monarchy."

"It's natural enough for Londoners to abhor the idea of violence against the Queen," agreed Daniel, "But why would they think the *London Illustrated Weekly* was to blame?"

"Because I am a supporter of the Chartists, as you know. In articles that I have written and that I have caused other people to write, I have freely stated my feelings that every man deserves a vote. There should be no property requirement for voting or for standing as a member in Parliament. The Queen and her advisers want to keep to the old ways, especially the Prime Minister. He has been accusing everyone associated with this newspaper of stirring up trouble."

"But surely no one will take that seriously. No one at this newspaper has ever attempted violence against the Queen or anyone else. Whoever fired the shot that killed the poor policeman must be a madman, like that other poor fellow who tried to kill the Queen a few weeks ago. No one in his right mind would take such a risk with so little chance of success."

"Don't be so sure," cautioned Reynolds, leaning across the table to whisper hoarsely to Daniel. "There are still many radicals about who want to start a revolution by inciting the government to violence. A few shots into a crowd, a few honest workmen killed and many people will be wild for revenge. Remember what happened in France not too long ago? Don't you believe that Englishmen can be roused to the same kind of revolutionary fervor as the French?"

"What do you think the newspaper ought to do? What can I do?"

"Find the men who were involved in the trouble at the Chartist demonstration. The police took their names. Those are the men who would have radical connections. One of them might know who would be willing to use violence to get a revolution started. The police are unlikely to do anything useful. This is an opportunity for our newspaper to prove it is on the side of justice, but does not support mindless violence."

Daniel felt torn. He wanted to find the culprit, but he was aware that he might put Tom in danger. Surely most of the other men who had been picked up at the demonstration were just as innocent as Tom was. How could he judge what trouble he might cause by investigating them? As Daniel left Reynolds and headed home for dinner, the London skies seemed more gray and threatening than ever. He walked quickly, eager to get home and talk to Charlotte. What would she think about Reynold's plan?

He found Charlotte in the kitchen unpacking a basket of vegetables. She had some of them spread out on the table and was writing the names down on a large sheet of paper.

"Are you doing that for your class?" asked Daniel. "You cannot stop being a teacher, can you?"

"No, it seems that I never will stop. There is so much that Betty and the other girls want to learn. I thought I could write down some recipes to help them learn to cook. If Deirdre and Kathleen are ever going to be more than scullery maids, they must learn to read recipes and to write shopping orders for tradesmen."

"Is it cooks they want to be? By the time they know enough to become cooks perhaps we will be rich enough to hire a cook of our own. Wouldn't you like that, Charlotte?"

"Indeed I would. And I am sure we will have a cook someday. But I don't need a cook right now. I have little enough to do and time hangs heavy when I have no work."

"Well both of us will have enough work to do now. Mr. Reynolds asked me to find the men who were at the demonstration and were brought into the police station for questioning. He thinks the guilty man might be someone who is trying to start a revolution. If we talk to some of those men we might be able to track down the man who shot the guard at Buckingham Palace before the police find him."

"You never told him about Tom, did you?"

"Of course I didn't. Tom is not a radical and he is certainly not someone who would try to shoot the Queen. But he was a fool to run away. That only makes him seem more guilty. I'd like to find him and talk some sense into him."

"We all want to find him. Poor Betty is beside herself with worry." Charlotte frowned as she tried to think of some way to find her brother.

"Perhaps when we start putting the stories about the radicals in our newspaper, Tom will hear about it and start thinking he should come back and straighten things out with the police."

"But he can't read, Daniel! He will never know there are stories in the newspaper about him unless someone reads them to him. I am sure he is hiding out on the streets and in the rookeries over by St. Giles. None of the people there pay the slightest attention to newspapers or to what the police are doing. The only thing they think of when they see a policeman is to run away and hide."

"Or sometimes they throw stones," Daniel added. "I've seen that happen too. But why don't we at least try to see whether we can find Tom? Where do you think he might have gone?"

"The only place in the city where he has ever stayed is in the doorway of that church that he and Betty sheltered in when they first came to London. We could walk over there and see if we can find someone who has seen him."

"I must go to work this afternoon, but we can walk there tomorrow. Tom should not be too hard to find.

With his red hair he stands out in a crowd," Daniel said hopefully, "so perhaps someone noticed him."

CHAPTER SIX

Visit to a Grieving Family

When Daniel returned to his office, he wanted to discover more about the man who had been killed. As usual, several men were waiting for him at the pub next door to his office. These were the hangers-on who hoped to win fame by submitting articles for the newspaper. They were hoping to get an assignment to write a story and were eager to give Daniel suggestions about what they could do.

"Lord Melbourne will be speaking in the Lord's chamber tonight," suggested one eager young man. "Shall I write a report on what he has to say about the situation in India? There is much disorder along the Afghanistan border, I hear, and General McNaughton cannot control the fighting among the natives."

"The Queen will be entertaining Lord and Lady Haverton to dinner this afternoon" chimed in another. "Our readers might like an account of what will be served at the royal table."

No one appeared to have any information about the slaying of the policeman at the Palace. The men who wrote for the *London News* were far more interested in talking with the aristocracy than with the commoners who worked for the police or investigated crimes. Policemen were not considered worth the attention of men of substance. Daniel had his own opinions about the dandified men who wanted to write about royal dinners, but he was careful not to express them. It was important to maintain good relationships with men of influence. He made up his mind to talk with the police himself.

At mid-afternoon the police station was likely to be quiet. Crimes were usually committed under cover of darkness and whoever might have been picked up during the night for being disorderly on the streets or attempting to rob a passer-by would probably be released in the morning.

The street peddlers were out in full force. Daniel noticed a young Italian boy with a large tray hung round his neck. He was charging a farthing for a view of the four white mice he had in a basket on the tray. Small children crowded around him trying to get a glimpse of the tiny creatures, but the boy was very strict about letting anyone see them before they had paid for the privilege. Daniel smiled to think that mice would cause such a stir in a city where rats and mice roamed through houses in every neighborhood.

At the police station, only a few men were on duty. Daniel asked for the sergeant in charge.

"Oh he's not here," one of the younger policemen told him. "He's gone to the wake for poor Sean Costello who was shot to death by some villain."

"Where is the wake? I would like to go and pay my respects."

"It's just round the corner near the Square at the White Kettle. You'll find quite a crowd there I'm sure. People around here are raring for the chance to avenge his death."

Daniel found the pub was indeed almost filled with people, men and women both, who were talking and arguing loudly as they drank pints of beer. In a quieter room out back, Sean Costello's body was laid out on a table. Two women in black mourning veils were standing close to it and accepting the condolences of visitors. Daniel walked over to pay his respects.

The older woman, clearly Sean Costello's mother, nodded her head gravely as Daniel told her how sorry he was about her loss. "And this is young Sean's wife", she said, introducing the younger woman. "And her expecting a baby this spring. Sure who would do such a terrible thing as fire a shot to kill me son?"

"But surely the shot wasn't meant for him."

"Well, if it was meant for the Queen then the man who shot it was a fool. Poor Sean was no closer to her than I am to the square. There's hard feelings against the police, you know. I think it might have been someone with a grudge against the force." Mrs. Costello stopped speaking and burst into sobs.

"Ah, what is this? My good lady you must not cry and despair. Your son died doing his duty, so God will take him to His bosom. We will all be called when the time comes."

Daniel hadn't noticed the man who came bustling in and was standing in front of Mrs. Costello peering intently at her. Everyone seemed to know him and a crowd soon formed around him. Daniel listened quietly to the excited chatter trying to find out who he might be. To his surprise, the young Mrs. Costello, Sean's wife, spoke up fearlessly.

"Mr. O'Connor, sir, your Chartist demonstration not long ago aroused a lot of protest against the police and my poor husband was shot because of that. My baby will be without a father. What do you think of that? All this talk of revolution and republicanism does nothing but cause us poor people to suffer. You should be ashamed of yourself, sir."

There were mutters of disagreement and nods of agreement in the crowd. Daniel realized the small man who had entered the room must be Feargus O'Connor, the famous member of Parliament who was always talking about the Irish question and demanding independence for his native country. A whole new set of questions and arguments were coming up now. The outspoken young Mrs. Costello was being lectured by an elderly man who insisted that her husband had died defending the Queen and would be rising to heaven immediately.

Feargus O'Connor raised his hands and shook them impatiently as more and more people crowded around him expressing their opinion about the Chartists, the Republicans, and the Queen.

"Forgive me, good people, I must leave you all and go to the House for the debate tonight. I stopped by merely to give my condolences to the family of the brave member of our London police force, Sean Costello. You must excuse me, I have work to do for our country."

One man seized his sleeve and tried to keep him from leaving immediately, but O'Connor turned angrily on him. "Unhand me, sir! I will not be treated like a criminal! Let me go on my way."

As the angry politician strode out the door, Daniel followed him. He hurried along beside him trying to keep up with the older man's pace. "Pardon me, sir. I do not wish to hinder your work or keep you from your important duties. I am a newspaperman and I would like to have an opportunity to ask your opinions on a number of important public questions."

O'Connor slowed down a bit and turned toward Daniel. "You can listen to my speeches in the House if you wish to know my opinions. I do not hide them. Who are you? What newspaper do you work for?"

"My name is Daniel Gallagher and I work with Mr. Reynolds on his *London Weekly Newspaper*. It is not only your opinions on important public issues that I would like to discuss. It is also the violence that has occurred in this city recently. I am Irish like yourself, but I have lived in America these past five years and have only recently returned from overseas. I have been surprised at the intemperate speech I have heard in this city and by the evidence of citizen unrest. The violence at your Chartist demonstration was disturbing and in recent weeks there have been several attacks on the Queen's life. That is not like the England I have heard about."

"Not all the trouble is caused by supporters of the Charter, young man." O'Connor glared at Daniel. "There's many a troublemaker in the pay of aristocrats who want to keep their privileges. All they do is goad honest working men to violence and try to sully the cause we are fighting for. As for the killing of the young policeman, I have heard from people who ought to know that it was the work of a madman."

They were almost at the Parliament building and Daniel knew he would have only a few more minutes to gain access to O'Connor's information. "Would it be possible for me to make an appointment to meet with you and hear your theories about why this disorder is spreading? Have foreign revolutionary forces from the continent come onto our shores? Where will it all end? Some people say there will be a revolution here as there was in France fifty years ago."

The Parliament buildings loomed above them when O'Connor glanced sharply at Daniel. "All right young man, you may see my secretary about making an appointment. I have always been a strong supporter of the right of newspapers to print stories about important news of the day. I hope your newspaper will not waste its time on gossip and chitchat about aristocrats but will pay attention to the issues that affect the people."

By the time they parted, Daniel was sure he would have a chance to find out what O'Connor's plans for the future were. He was no closer, however, to discovering why young Sean Costello had been shot. And both Charlotte and Betty would be bitterly disappointed when he came home with no news about where Tom might be hiding.

Although he was tired and hungry, he turned to walk again past St Barnabas, the church where Tom and Betty had sheltered when they first arrived in the city. The church was not locked so Daniel went inside and looked around. St Barnabas was a High Anglican church and looked very much like the Catholic churches Daniel had seen during his boyhood in Ireland, although the stained glass windows were grander and the candlesticks on the altar gleamed more brightly.

A few people were sitting in the pews, most, Daniel suspected, just looking for a place to sit down and rest. He inspected each one as he walked slowly toward the altar. A movement to his right caught his eye and he turned in time to see a red-haired man walking swiftly toward the door Daniel had just entered. Could that be Tom? Had he seen Daniel and run away?

Daniel turned quickly back to the door and hurried onto the street as fast as he could. He pushed his way through some peddlers and an actor showing off a dancing monkey. There was no sign of any red-haired men. Slowly Daniel gave up and turned toward home.

CHAPTER SEVEN

Invitation to a Museum

The next morning when Daniel went to the office, he tried to put Tom out of his mind and concentrate on preparing the newspaper. Not long after he started selecting the articles that would be used in this week's edition, Mr. Reynolds arrived.

"There is to be a reception at the British Museum tomorrow," Reynolds announced. "The occasion is the installation of the Payava tomb, an ancient relic, which the distinguished archeologist Charles Fellows found in Turkey. He is presenting it to the British government and I think we should have a story about how this treasure is enriching all Britons."

"Do you think many people care about ancient remains from the Middle East?" asked Daniel skeptically. "Most people are concerned with their own poverty and not with the riches of foreign countries in the East. And right now they are concerned about who shot the young policeman at the Palace."

"Ah," exclaimed Reynolds. "At least that mystery appears to be solved. The police have apprehended an eccentric man, a hunchback, who appears to be completely mad. His response to questions is to mutter that Caesar must be killed and that he is fighting for the rights of all Romans."

"How is it that these madmen get guns? Twice now the Queen has been threatened by people who did not know what they were doing. Well, it is lucky that the man has been taken off the streets, but we don't want to forget all of the unrest in this country. That is what breeds these crimes. The next time such a threat occurs it might be from an organized plot against the Queen."

"I agree," Reynolds said. "What we need is reform. When every man has a vote and feels himself a part of the country, then people will cease the violence and will begin to care about culture and history. We are entering a new era and soon it will be every man, not only aristocrats, who are walking through the halls of the British Museum. Our newspaper must enlighten people about the treasures of London as well as the poverty and crime."

On the day of the reception, Charlotte put on her best dress and she and Daniel set out for the museum. As they walked up the steps and through the tall columns at the entrance, Charlotte murmured to Daniel, "I can understand why many people would be afraid of coming here. The building is terribly grand and not very welcoming. I am glad you have your assignment from Mr. Reynolds, so no one will dare turn us away. I am sure Tom and Betty would be too frightened to walk up these steps."

A tall guard dressed in black pointed the way toward a gallery where a small crowd was gathered. Several large sculptures were scattered around the room behind the glass-covered cases that held a variety of small exotic objects. Charlotte's eyes swept over the crowd as she moved slowly along the row of cases. There were very few women in the group, but Charlotte was delighted to see that one of them was the familiar figure of Margaret Fuller, someone she had known when she lived in Massachusetts. She was proud of being on friendly terms with one of the most famous writers in America. Although she knew Miss Fuller was on a European tour, she had not expected to meet her in London.

Charlotte moved toward Miss Fuller to pay her respects, but hesitated as she saw that her friend was engaged in a lively conversation with a tall, bearded man. Just then Miss Fuller turned, noticed Charlotte hesitating, and beckoned her closer,

"I would like to introduce you to George Scharf, the artist who painted scenes of the expedition that brought these treasures back to the museum. Mr. Scharf, this is Mrs. Gallagher, a friend of mine from Boston days. Like me, she is enjoying her first trip to London. Perhaps you have time to explain a few of these items to us."

The artist was happy to talk about the antiquities in the cases nearby. As he spoke, pointing out intricate carvings on some daggers and the jewels set into others, a small group of people gathered around to listen. One tall young man with a military bearing and a jet-black mustache seemed particularly interested. Finally he spoke up.

"Ah, I have seen some of these weapons still in use in the East. When I was in the service of the Queen in India, we came across a number of fellows who were well-versed in the use of these scimitars—devilishly sharp they are too."

"Yes, they are effective weapons. But here, as you see, the collection includes not only weapons but also adornments and even religious tokens. This remarkable piece is a Khanda, a form that has great significance for some groups."

Charlotte recognized the form from the picture Kumar Singh had drawn of the jewel stolen from his family. The piece in the museum was made of metal, not a jewel, but it was a striking object nonetheless.

The military man was speaking again. "Oh yes, I believe the Sikhs worship this little form. But then, the heathen Indians worship all sorts of things. What can we expect of such people? They will never become civilized Englishmen. I don't know why we put their heathen tokens in our great museum."

Soon after that the group broke up and Charlotte had time to talk to Margaret Fuller by herself. She told Miss

Fuller about how she was teaching Betty and some of the immigrant girls how to read. "The poor young immigrants suffer because they have no way of getting in touch with their families. Trying to find someone to write a letter is difficult."

"Oh yes," Miss Fuller agreed. "So many of the immigrants here are cut off completely from their families. One of my friends has started a school for the young Italian boys who come here to earn a living by being peddlers or street performers. These young workers should be taught the skills they need to find decent jobs and provide for themselves and their families. Teaching them is difficult work and takes a great deal of patience, because the youngsters work such long hours just to get enough to eat."

"The young women I teach, and perhaps the boys, understand that they need education," Charlotte agreed, "but there is so much anger and revolutionary fervor among many of the English men that I wonder whether they will think schools are enough. Many people appear to prefer starting a revolution."

"The American Revolution succeeded in building a new country, but that was led by educated men. Do you think the Chartists and other revolutionaries in England have the wisdom to devise a republic? The more education people have, the wiser their politics will be. You and I should talk about these things, but alas I travel on to Paris tomorrow and will not be back in London for several months."

With those closing words, Margaret Fuller was swept away by her host to speak with other guests. Soon afterward Charlotte and Daniel started home. Charlotte described to him what the artist had said about the antiquities in the cases.

"There was a military man there—at least he said he had served the Queen in India—who seemed knowledgeable about Eastern antiquities, but quite scornful of the Indian people.

"Do you mean the man with the remarkable mustache?" Daniel asked. "His name is Captain Granville, I believe. I spoke with him for a few minutes to get some details for my story."

"But wasn't that the name of the man Mr. Singh mentioned as helping him to get an interview with the Queen?" asked Charlotte. "This man does not sound as though he is at all sympathetic toward Indians. In fact he was quite scornful. Why would he want to help Kumar Singh?"

Charlotte puzzled over that question as they walked home. The reception had given her a great deal to think about. She was happy that Margaret Fuller approved of her teaching. It was exciting to talk about starting a new school and speculating about a possible revolution, but they had not yet discovered who had attacked the guard at the palace. How could she and Daniel accomplish all of the things they hoped for? Charlotte sighed deeply as she prepared for bed.

In the days that followed, Charlotte began to sink back into the bleak gray mood that had gripped her during her first days in London. The weather turned colder, chilly drops of rain dripped relentlessly from the sky. After Betty and Daniel had left for their work, Charlotte sat in the kitchen huddled close to the warmth of the kitchen fire. The effort of building a fire in the parlor seemed too much to handle. She knew she should not brood over how long it would take to change conditions in England. Teaching a few young women to read was such a small ambition. And what if she and Daniel could never build a better life here in London? Never be able to do anything really important? What would happen to their dreams of a better life? The future looked bleak and hopeless.

In desperation she picked up one of the books she had been teaching Betty to read, Dickens's *Pickwick Papers*. After ten minutes of reading, she thought she heard the postman's step at the door, she ran upstairs to collect the mail feeling almost cheerful. She and Daniel seldom received mail; surely there must be good news. A letter from one of their American friends would change the gloomy aspect of the day.

But the single letter that dropped through the mail slot was not from America. Charlotte looked searchingly at the unknown handwriting. The envelope bore no stamp, so it must have been delivered by hand and probably came from someone nearby. It could have been from someone at Daniel's newspaper, but the name on the envelope was Mrs. Daniel Gallagher. Quickly she opened it.

My dear Mrs. Gallagher,

I take the liberty of asking a great favor of you. When you and your husband kindly invited my husband and me to take tea with you, we were very impressed by your experience as a teacher. As you may remember, I told you that I have led a very quiet life, secluded from all society except for my family. I was given only the domestic education considered suitable for a girl. Here in England, I have no contact with my family; therefore I have no friends with whom to spend time. Although I can read, my education has been limited and I am not able to understand and fully appreciate the books and newspapers that my husband likes to read and discuss.

As you can understand, the lack of friends and of occupation, occasionally make me feel very sad. You told me that we could become friends and I would like that very much. I wonder whether you might call upon me and spend some time conversing and learning. You could teach me about the world outside of India.

Perhaps, because you are an experienced teacher you could also teach my servant Parni to read. I can help you. Oh, I can dream of many things we can do together as teachers and friends.

If you would be willing to call upon me, would you please send a note suggesting a day and a time. My husband will be pleased to provide an escort to bring you to our home.

Meena Kaur

Charlotte replied quickly to the note and told Meena Kaur that she would be glad to call and that she would not need an escort to walk such a short distance during the daylight.

The note had put her into a more cheerful mood, and her thoughts turned to her brother Tom. He had not been seen for almost a week. Surely if her brother knew that someone else had admitted he was the one who had shot the policeman, Tom would have returned. She knew Betty worried that something bad had happened to him. Charlotte had scoffed at the idea, but she was beginning to think Betty might be right. Her young brother might have been injured. He might have been arrested. She would have to do something to find him.

The weather outside was still drizzly and cold. The sky had been so dark all day that Charlotte couldn't tell whether darkness was falling or whether she would have a few more hours of semi-daylight. Nonetheless, she pulled on her heavy shawl and went out again. She would revisit the church where Tom and Betty had spent their first few days in London. At least she knew Tom was familiar with that area and might revisit it.

As she walked through the soggy streets toward the church, Charlotte wondered again whether Tom knew a man had been arrested. There had been stories in the newspaper, but Tom would not have seen those. Finally she saw St. Barnabas church looming ahead of her. She could see no one huddled around the doorway, but she plodded on toward the steps. Suddenly, there he was! That surely was Tom, walking toward the church from the other direction. She ran toward him.

"Tom, Tom, we have been so worried about you. Why didn't you come home? Betty is beside herself."

"Oh Charlotte, I have wanted to go back to your house, but I don't want to cause you and your husband any more trouble. How is Betty? I miss her terribly. I don't think I can stand it."

"But you are not in any more trouble, are you?" Charlotte peered at him anxiously. "The police came by the house once, but they have not returned and they have arrested someone else. Didn't you hear that news? Why must you stay away from us? Are you living on the streets? Have you found work?"

"I've found work enough unloading cargo from the river boats. Enough to feed myself, but not to pay for lodgings, so I've been living rough this past week. I've met a lot of radicals who say the police have been questioning people. There are stories about looking for a hunchback. I didn't know what to think. There are bad things going on here in the city."

"Well, come back with me to see Betty. I have plenty of food in the house for a good warm meal. We can talk about what you have been doing after you've had a chance to eat and wash up." Charlotte led the way back to Cecil Court.

When Daniel and Betty both got back to the house that evening, they were surprised to see Tom, cleaned up and wearing one of Daniel's jackets, sitting in front of the kitchen fire while Charlotte made tea. Daniel shook his hand, clapped him on the shoulder, and welcomed him, but Betty was less restrained. She burst into tears and kept hugging Tom and hanging onto him as though she was afraid he would try to leave again. Over and over again she said, "You must stay here. You must never leave me again." Finally they all settled down to eat.

After the meal Tom told his story haltingly, looking a little shamefaced. "I am a countryman, as you know, and this big city is too confusing and too wicked for me. When I thought the police might pick me up again and accuse me of shooting one of their men, my only thought was to hide. I almost started walking back toward Bristol, but the weather was so bad the road was impossible. Anyway I didn't have any food and I didn't want to go too far from Betty. I knew I wanted to get back to her as soon as I could.

"So I walked down to the quayside where I had worked before and found some work on one of the ships. I unloaded cargo all day, which didn't give me much time to think. Afterwards I had no place to go and I walked over to a pub with one of the men who'd been working with me. Jock was his name. He said he was from up North—Lancashire I think he said.

"We had a pint of beer and a plate of eels and he told me what he and some of his friends were planning. 'We don't need the Queen' he said, 'nor her foreign husband neither. The rich folks keep all the money while people like you and me slave away on the dock. We need a republic, just like the rebels in America have. They got rid of the old king and I say we should get rid of the new queen'."

"When he said he and his friends would do this, what did he mean?" asked Daniel. "Was he talking about an organized group or just a few friends?"

"Ah, I don't rightly know what he meant, but I knew he was steamed up about it. He bought me another pint of beer and we sat there for a long time comfortable as could be. Although I was thinking of you, Betty" he added quickly.

"Have you seen Jock again?" asked Charlotte. "Is he planning to do anything to get a republic?"

"Lots of people have a lot of ideas. And some of them I am sworn to keep secret. It's a long story."

"Well, we will have time to hear it. I know you are tired now, Tom, but you are my brother and we must stick together. You and Betty had better stay on with us a while longer until things settle down."

CHAPTER EIGHT

Meeting the Ladies

In a day or two Tom had settled easily back into the household routine. And then it was time for Charlotte's visit to the Singh's house. As she walked there on Tuesday afternoon, she wondered what the household would look like. Would the furniture be in the familiar English style or would there be rugs and cushions on the floor like the ones she had seen in paintings of the East? And would the Singhs serve the familiar English tea or some exotic Indian drink?

The man who answered the door when Charlotte rang was dressed, as Kumar Singh dressed, in a dark suit of the British style. On his head he wore a white turban, but unlike his master he was clean shaven and had neither mustache nor beard. He led Charlotte to the parlor and threw open the door. The first sight that greeted them was an ornate ceramic stove that radiated warmth through the room. The floor was covered with several crimson, soft green and brown carpets, strewn across the floor. On the floor in front of the stove were three or four large cushions; Charlotte noticed a purple one, a yellow striped one and another that mingled red and blue flowers in an complicated pattern.

Next to the stove were several typical British chairs and in one of them sat Meena Kaur, wearing a brightly patterned green tunic with touches of blue and wide-legged blue and red trousers. She stood up as Charlotte entered and walked toward the door to welcome her. She clasped her hands together as though she were about to pray, and bowed her head slightly toward Charlotte and said, "Welcome to our home. Thank you for your visit."

Meena Kaur looked more relaxed than she had when she visited Charlotte and Daniel in their home. She seemed even younger, certainly no more than nineteen or twenty years old. On her feet were sandals of braided leather with pearls entwined with the strands. Over her head, instead of a turban, she had thrown a sheer rose-colored scarf that blended with the flowing lines of her garment.

"Will you please sit down," she invited Charlotte. "My maid will soon serve tea. Our cook is English, so we are able to offer you food to which you are accustomed. I believe you are the first English person who has ever visited our home." She seemed delighted at the event.

Charlotte was even more charmed by Meena than she had been the first time they met. Within a few minutes, the two of them were talking comfortably together. The servant girl who brought the tea looked like a younger version of Meena; Charlotte guessed she could not be more than fourteen or fifteen years old. She was dressed in clothes similar to her mistress, but they were made of coarse cotton and the colors were rather harsh.

As the two women sipped their tea, Meena continued to talk. "Let me tell you some of the ideas I have been turning over in my mind since I met you and your husband. You are a teacher and I admire your work with some of the young women here in London. My maid, Parni, has never learned to read and I would be most grateful if you would add her to your class. In fact, I have come up with a scheme that I think you might find helpful for you and your students.

"As you can see, my husband had taken a rather large house here in London, and we have many rooms—far more than we can use. We have not yet been blessed with children, so I have a great deal of time. We could provide you with a classroom for your school and supplies of paper and books. In return we would like you to teach Parni to read and perhaps some of the maids in other Indian families. Several gentlemen in this city have started what they call ragged schools for working boys, but we do not like the idea of girls being taught in the same room as boys. All of your students, I believe, are young women, are they not?"

"Yes, they are," Charlotte reassured her.

Meena clapped her hands together in pleasure. "My parents were careful to give me a good education. They employed tutors to teach me English and French, but they did not think a girl needed to know anything about history or other important subjects. I learned the stories of Indian history, but I know almost nothing about Europe. If I could help you in your work, I would learn so much. I have never had a friend outside of my family. It would be a true blessing to have an English friend!"

Meena showed Charlotte the room they could use for the school. It was a large dining room with a massive table in the center and six chairs lined up on either side. There would be room for many students and to put a desk at the head of the table for the teacher. Charlotte had never seen such lavish fittings for a school room. The walls were adorned with portraits of the ancestors of the man who had built the house a century before.

Charlotte went home later that afternoon thinking about how she could teach girls from India along with Betty and her friends who wanted to learn how to read. The English and Irish girls would have heard the folktales that Charlotte had used to teach them to read, but would they mean anything to Parni and the other Indian women? Still, some of the nursery rhymes would appeal to anyone and talked about situations everyone could understand.

Cobbler, cobbler, mend my shoe,

Give it a stitch and that will do.
Here's a nail, and there's a prod,
And now my shoe is well shod.

And she could use Bible verses. But the Singhs were not Christian. Perhaps she had better stay away from Bible verses. Some of the innocent songs that Mr. Blake had written could surely be used by someone of any religion:

Little Lamb who made thee?
 Dost thou know who made thee?
Gave thee life & bid thee feed.
By the stream & o'er the mead;
Gave thee clothing of delight,
Softest clothing wooly bright;
Gave thee such a tender voice,
Making all the vales rejoice?

Teaching people to read sounded like an excellent idea, but Charlotte could see there might be a great many problems doing it. Still, it was better than just sitting at home and worrying. She would devise lessons for her new pupils just as she had for the boys and girls she taught at Brook Farm and for the free black children in New York.

On Monday morning Charlotte went back to the Singh's house to meet her new class. Meena had gathered six young women. They were seated at the long dining room table smiling timidly. All of them wore long flowing clothes in bright colors. Two wore green and yellow flower prints and the others shades of red.

Charlotte and Meena sat at the head of the table. "All of these women have learned some English," Meena said, "but they do not often have a chance to practice. I will translate for you and for them if there are difficulties in understanding."

Charlotte looked around the table and asked each of the women to say her name. She tried to write down each name, but they were so unfamiliar that she lost track. She would have to learn them slowly and practice them as time went by.

"Have any of you been to school before?" she asked. The women looked at her shyly but for several minutes no one said anything. Finally the oldest in the group spoke up, "I went to a village school when I was a child, but I was so afraid of the teacher that I couldn't learn much. She beat us whenever we made a mistake."

"There will be no beating in this class," Charlotte promised. "You will all have a chance to practice English and to learn how to read and write."

Charlotte showed the women the alphabet she had written out and they each started to copy a letter and then read it aloud to the group. Meena had provided them each with a slate on which they wrote their letter and then read them proudly to the group. Charlotte could see that it was a struggle for them and as they became tired, they slipped more and more into their native language and stopped trying to speak English.

After an hour's work, Charlotte decided they needed a change, so she sang a few nursery songs with them. They enjoyed learning "Twinkle, twinkle little star" so she was encouraged to try another one. "Do you know what a Ladybird is?" she asked. "Those little flying insects that flash a light as they fly? Here is a song about them."

Ladybird! Ladybird!
Fly away home.
Your house is on fire.
And your children all gone.

While most of the Indian women smiled and sang along, Meena shrank into her chair looking miserable and her maid, Parni, pulled her scarf over her face.

"Please, please, do not talk about fire! Oh, this class must be over. These women must leave."

The other women rose obediently and prepared to leave the house. Charlotte was bewildered, but she didn't want to frighten the women, so she spoke in a calm voice. "You have been good scholars today and we have done a great deal of work. Try to remember your letters and practice them when you get home."

She ushered the class members toward the door and the Indian manservant appeared to give them their cloaks and send them on their way. Meena and her maid darted into the parlor and Charlotte followed them to say goodbye and thank her hostess.

There was still a fire burning in the stove and Charlotte noted that did not seem to frighten either of the women. But the fire was safely contained in the hollow of the large ceramic stove and Meena sat several feet away in a luxurious velvet chair. Parni crouched at her feet like a child. Both of them appeared shaken.

"I am sorry that the little song I sang about the ladybird disturbed you," Charlotte apologized. "It is just a nursery song that children sing in my country. If I had thought it would offend you, I never would have used it. I hope you will forgive me."

By this time Meena was sitting up straighter in her chair and appeared calmer than she had been. "No, no, it is I who must apologize. It was the thought of fire that frightened me. You could not know my history. I will tell you how I came to be so afraid of fire.

"About five years ago, when I was still a young girl, I lived with my parents in a large house in Amritsar. It was a comfortable life because my father was a great leader and we had many jewels and luxuries. Parni was given to me as my servant when she was eight years old and she followed me everywhere and did whatever I asked of her. Like my mother and other women, of course, I could not go outside of our house and grounds except on occasions of great celebration or holiday. We lived quiet and sheltered lives and knew of no dangers.

"But there were dangers. My father, as I have said, was a great leader and he was opposed by a powerful general who wanted to become the ruler of our province. One night he and his men attacked our compound. They stole into the palace and seized gold and jewels. When my father's manservant tried to defend the family, he was slaughtered. My father avenged his life with his sword and the attacker was slain. Other men in the group set fire to the house before they fled.

"Cowards that they were, they set fire to the women's quarters. Oh, I will never forget the screams of terror when we discovered what had happened. A great flaming beam fell from the ceiling and my clothes started to burn. My brave mother wrapped me in a blanket to put out the flames and pushed me out of danger. My brothers helped us escape from the house, but the fire has left me scarred and unable to walk easily. My poor mother suffered so much from the horror and the deaths of so many of our servants that she died of the shock of it two years later.

"I have been very lucky because my father gave me to Kumar Singh as a bride and he has been very good to me. And my little Parni survived and has come with me all the way to this strange land of England. But sometimes when I am reminded of the past, I become very frightened. For many years I have had dreams of fire. The memory of that night will never leave me."

CHAPTER NINE

Fire! Fire!

The sun barely lightened the morning sky on Thursday when Deirdre set out from her lodgings to start her work as scullery maid in the Singh kitchen. A light rain was falling and she clutched her shawl around her as she hurried down the gray street. She and the kitchen maid always lit the fire in the kitchen the first thing in the morning. They needed hot water for tea and for cooking breakfast for the household. The kitchen maid, like the cook, lived in the house and she frequently complained that Deirdre was late.

"But the clock says you are half an hour late," she scolded as Deirdre gathered coals for the fire. Deirdre looked at the small kitchen clock uncomprehendingly. No matter how hard she tried, she had never learned to read the numbers and figure out the correct time. If only all clocks had chimes the way the large grandfather clock in Mr. Singh's parlor did, she could count the number. But the bland face of the clock kitchen clock told her nothing. All she could do was stand in dumb silence and listen to the angry mutter of the kitchen maid.

After breakfast had been served in the shabby but still-elegant dining room, Deirdre had the task of scrubbing plates and pans while the cook and the kitchen maid went to the market to buy food for dinner. She walked out to the yard to pump water for the kitchen and carried the bucket back indoors to splash into the tin dish tub. Heating the water took a long time and Deirdre sighed as she thought of the work ahead of her, preparing vegetables for dinner, clearing out the fireplaces. Oh how she wished she was still at home with her mother in County Down instead of here in this godforsaken city.

She tried to cheer herself up by singing a song she had heard a young Irish lad singing on the street a few days before

Oh, Mary, this London's a wonderful sight,
With people all working by day and by night.
Sure they don't sow potatoes, nor barley, nor wheat,
But there's gangs of them digging for gold in the street.
At least when I asked them that's what I was told,
So I just took a hand at this digging for gold,
But for all that I found there I might as well be
Where the Mountains of Mourne sweep down to the sea.

As she was crooning the words softly to herself, she heard someone banging at the kitchen door. Another peddler coming by no doubt, not that she had any money to buy so much as a ribbon for her hair. She stepped outside to shoo the man away, but he was determined to come into the kitchen.

"I must speak to the master of the house," the man said. His voice was loud and clear as if he might be a policeman. He seemed very sure Deirdre would obey him.

"I'm only the scullery maid, sir," said Deirdre. "Sure the master would pay no attention to me. He has scarcely ever seen my face."

"Do as I say!" The man moved toward her threateningly. "Don't talk back to your betters. Just run upstairs and tell Mr. Singh I must talk to him."

Deirdre cowered near the door, but then turned and plodded upstairs toward the parlor. She looked down the hallway and saw no one there. Mr. Singh must still be in the parlor. The house was not large enough to require many servants. The manservant who had come with Kumar Singh took care of his personal needs, while the kitchen staff worked downstairs and did most of the cleaning in the small set of rooms. Deirdre knew Mr. Singh's wife lived up on the third floor, but she never came to the kitchen. She had an Indian serving girl to act as her maid and Deirdre almost never saw Mrs. Singh except as an occasional flash of exotic clothing on the stairway. She would not dare go up to the third floor to find her.

Deirdre knocked on the parlor door and listened as hard as she could while she waited for an answer. Hearing nothing, she slowly pushed the door open and peeped in. The morning newspaper was lying on a table next to a large comfortable chair, but there was no sign of anyone in the room. Mr. Singh must have left the house already and taken his manservant with him.

Feeling giddy with relief that she did not have to confront the master, Deirdre hurried downstairs to tell the mysterious peddler that his call was in vain. But the man was nowhere to be seen. The kitchen was empty. Not a soul in sight, but a strange chemical smell pervaded the air.

As she turned toward the kitchen fire, she gasped. The small fire she had left had grown into an inferno. Someone had thrown something—hay was it?—that had blazed up. And the strange smell was stronger now.

Deirdre grabbed the pail of water she had brought in for the dishes and ran toward the fire to dowse the flames. One pail of water had little effect and she realized she would have to go out and pump some more, but as she turned to go, her skirt suddenly flamed up.

Desperately she beat the flames with her hands and with the empty pail she was holding. The pain engulfed her and screams tore out of her throat. Looking around desperately for something to quench the flame she tried to tear the dress from her body, but her hands were already blistered and she could not pull the heavy fabric away. She stumbled toward the door trying to get to the well outside, but as she opened the door, flames caught the back of her dress and her screams turned into incoherent moans of agony as she fell to the floor.

An unpleasant chemical smell still hung over the kitchen when the cook and the kitchen maid returned from market and wisps of smoke were drifting up from the kitchen fire.

"Holy Mother of God! What's happened here?" gasped Molly, the kitchen maid, as she entered.

The cook bent over Deirdre's charred body and touched her gently. "Ah, the poor child is gone," she sighed. "How did she ever catch her dress on fire. It's only a small fire. I've told her time and time again to be careful. She had no right to be so careless. What will the master say?"

When Kumar Singh and his manservant returned, they too shuddered at the bizarre accident. Singh contacted the local police and fire brigades, but there was nothing to be done. The house was scarcely damaged. Only Deirdre's terrible fate had turned the event into a tragedy.

The police were inclined to dismiss the accident as just another example of an Irish immigrant being careless and bringing trouble on herself. They paid no attention to the lingering chemical odor.

"No crime has been committed here," said one of them. "It's no business of ours if an ignorant scullery maid kills herself with a fire."

"But this was no accident," Singh insisted. "You can recognize the smell surely. It is ether, that new gas which doctors have started using to kill pain when they amputate limbs or assist at births. There was no ether in this house. Someone must have deliberately tried to turn the kitchen fire into a deadly blaze."

"Did anyone see the man who did it?" asked the policeman.

"Molly and me was out doing the marketing," said the cook. "We left Deirdre here to wash the breakfast dishes and clear up the kitchen. We wasn't anywhere near the house when the fire started."

"And where were you, sir, when the fire started?" The policeman turned toward Singh.

"I went down to the Houses of Parliament to seek an appointment with the Member from this area. My manservant was with me to hold the umbrella should the rain increase. But now that you ask, I think perhaps I did see a man who might have been up to no good. As we walked down the street, we saw a tradesman with drive his wagon up the street. He stopped at our house and appeared to enter the area by the kitchen. I wonder whether he was the culprit. I should have asked him his business."

"It would have done no good, sir, if you had. He would hardly have told you what he was planning. And he may have done nothing. I still believe the fire was an accident. You had best tell the girl's family to take away the body and have an end to it. The police don't have time to track down an innocent man who was just selling his vegetables. What's needed here is not the police, but a gravedigger."

Kumar Singh was incensed by their unconcern. He understood that kitchen maids were like the lower caste people in India, unimportant and soon forgotten after their deaths. But he had expected more from the English justice system he had heard so much about. Perhaps the best place to find justice would be in a newspaper office rather than from the ranks of the police.

After the cook sent Molly off to find Deirdre's sister and tell her the tragic news, Kumar Singh instructed his manservant find a gravedigger and arrange to pay for the girl's burial. He knew very little about how Christians buried their dead, but he was sure there was some ceremony that should be held to commemorate the young woman whose life had been cut off while she was barely out of childhood.

After he had arranged the practical details, Kumar Singh went upstairs to speak to his wife. He sighed as he walked up the steep staircase. Poor Meena had grown quiet and sad since they had come to London. She was no longer the lively young girl he had married just two years ago. Meeting Mrs. Gallagher had helped but would she ever take her place as the center of the household as his mother had been? And now he had to give her news that would make her even more sad and frightened. He walked slowly up the steps.

Half an hour later, he was on the street heading toward the office of the *London Illustrated Weekly* and pondering how he could discover what had truly happened in the kitchen that morning. He knew he had enemies. The men from the East India Company had tangled with his guru, Ranjet Singh, and they had no wish to see the influence of his followers extended after his death. But why would a merchant engage in this bizarre criminal act? Did they want to burn the entire house down? Was he the target? It seemed the most likely explanation, but what was the gain for them?

He was glad to find that Daniel was in his office and was quite willing to talk. "I have a tragic story to tell you," Kumar Singh began. "A young Irish girl who works in my kitchen, Deidre O'Reilly is her name, died in a kitchen fire this morning."

"Deirdre O'Reilly did you say? I believe that my wife has been teaching that young woman to read these last several weeks. Like so many Irish immigrants she had very little schooling. Mrs. Gallagher and all the other women too will be shocked and sad to hear she has been killed. How did the accident happen?"

"No one else was near the kitchen at the time. My wife and her servant, Parni, stay up on the third floor during the morning until at least noon. They are too far from the kitchen to hear any noise or smell smoke from there. According to the cook, she and the other kitchen maid had left the house to go to the market. Deirdre was left to clean up the breakfast dishes. While the others were out, she somehow must have come too close to the fire and her clothing was set alight. By the time the others returned the poor girl was dead. The police seem to think she was just so ignorant and careless that she set herself on fire, but there was something very strange about the scene.

"The kitchen smelled of a chemical. I believe it was ether. Are you familiar with that new chemical? I have heard that it has been used by doctors to relieve pain in surgery and for women in childbirth. It has a very distinctive odor. I could smell it in the kitchen when I went down there. We keep no ether in the house."

"But why would a kitchen maid have ether? Why would she have used it? It is highly flammable I believe. Do you think she used it to make the fire brighter? I have never heard of anyone doing that. Most women are deadly afraid of chemicals." Daniel was bewildered trying to take in all the information.

"You may think me a fool, Mr. Gallagher, but I believe someone deliberately threw ether on the fire to start a conflagration. I think he may have wanted to burn the house down and me in it. Or perhaps he only wanted to frighten me into leaving London. We Sikhs have enemies and I have angered some powerful men. No one would have wanted to kill a poor Irish serving girl, but I believe someone was trying to injure me."

"Do you have any evidence? How could one of your enemies have entered your kitchen and poured ether on the fire? The police would never believe such a story."

"They would certainly not believe that story coming from me—one of the despised Indians they think so little of—but as I was leaving the house, shortly before this happened, I saw a peddler in a wagon stop outside my kitchen doorway. I think it is possible the man could have tricked that young girl into letting him enter the house. No one else was there and so he could have done his terrible deed and escaped without being seen." Kumar Singh clenched his fists as he talked.

"What do you want me to do?" asked Daniel.

"I would like you to investigate this crime and discover whether there is any truth in what I suspect. Perhaps my fate is not very important to the British government, but if someone or some group is trying to cause a war between the English and the Indians there may be many lives in danger. A newspaper man is an investigator, is he not? Will you try to discover the mystery at the heart of this tragedy?"

CHAPTER TEN

Searching

Daniel's pace slowed as he walked closer to home. He dreaded telling Charlotte what had happened. She had been so painfully sad when they first arrived in London. Now that she had met the Singhs and started teaching Betty and the other women to read, she was becoming more like her old self again. But something as terrible as Deirdre's tragedy could cast her back into the despair of their son's death. Poor Deirdre! The thought of how the girl must of suffered as the flames engulfed her dress was painful to think about. He had scarcely known the girl, but he felt the shock and distress of her loss. Deirdre had reminded him of his own sisters and he shuddered to think of her suffering. What kind of man could try to burn down a house and all the people in it?

Charlotte was seated at the kitchen table writing words on a large sheet of paper for her class to practice. When she saw Daniel, she jumped from her chair recognizing that something bad had happened. "What is it, Daniel? What is the matter?"

"I have terrible news for you and Betty."

"Oh, it's about Tom!"

"No, no. Not Tom. But a tragedy occurred in Kumar Singh's house. There was a kitchen fire and your friend Deirdre O'Reilly's skirt caught fire."

"Was she badly burned?"

"Worse than that. She was killed. It seems someone had thrown ether on the fire, which caused it to blaze up in deadly flames."

"Could no one help the girl?"

"Kumar Singh and his manservant were out for the morning and the cook and kitchen maid had gone to the market. Everything must have occurred very quickly." Slowly Daniel recounted the story of what had happened to Deirdre. Charlotte sat down again at the table and clenched her hands in her lap as she listened to the dreadful details. There was a long silence after Daniel had finished, but finally Charlotte spoke.

"Do you really think this was done on purpose? Surely no one would have wanted to injure Deirdre. She is very new to the city—new to this country. She knows almost no one here."

"I do not think it was the girl who was the cause of this. Whoever started that fire probably wanted to frighten and perhaps injure Kumar Singh. That is what he himself thinks. He says he has enemies who believe that Indians are trying to undermine the Empire. Mr. Singh might be a threat to them if he ever gets the ear of the Queen or one of her ministers. I have promised to help him find out what happened."

"Oh, Daniel, how are we to do that? Where would we start? London is a huge city. There must be thousands of people who want to cause trouble for the government. The only clue we have is the mysterious peddler Mr. Singh says he saw. Did anyone else see him? How could we track him down?"

Their talk was interrupted when Betty returned exhausted from her work as a laundress. It paid better than helping the barrow woman in the market, as she had proudly told Charlotte when she started, but the work was backbreaking. That morning, as every other day, she had picked up several loads of laundry from households in the neighborhood and carried them in a large basin to the public laundry. There she boiled water, scrubbed each piece of each load clean, and pushed each one through a wringer to squeeze out as much water as possible. Then each load had to be carried back to the house it came from. There she hung the laundry on lines strung across the kitchen or cellar so the pieces could finally dry. It was slow work drying clothes in soggy London weather. Only when that was done was she free to walk home and to rub her red, chapped hands with goose grease to ease the pain of their raw bleeding.

Charlotte hated to add to her burden by telling her what had happened to Deirdre, but it would be worse to delay the news. Betty crumbled in her chair as she listened and then put her head down in her arms and sobbed painfully. Charlotte held her shoulders and tried to ease the pain. Eventually Betty started to speak.

"Deirdre were so sure she would earn money and help her mother and father. Working in that kitchen was a blessing because she would get pay regular and not be out on the street trying to sell things. And you were teaching her to read—she was so happy about that. She worked hard, didn't she? She wanted to become a lady like you. Now she'll never be able to do anything, not anything at all." Betty's voice became a wail. "What are we going to tell her mother? What's going to become of her sister Kathleen? She's not more than half-grown. She'll not be able to live without Deirdre."

That reminded Charlotte that her work wasn't finished yet. Having taken on Deirdre and Kathleen as students, she had an obligation to them. After getting directions from Betty, she and Daniel set out to find Kathleen's room and make sure she would be all right for a few days at least. Betty wanted to come with them, but Charlotte insisted that she must stay and get some rest. Tomorrow would be another long, hard day of work.

Charlotte gently coaxed Kathleen out of the small, dark room she had shared with Deirdre and persuaded her to come back to stay with the Gallaghers while they arranged Deirdre's funeral. It was a simple enough ceremony. A young priest at St. Joseph's Church, which served many of the Irish in London, performed a funeral service and Kumar Singh provided a coffin for Deirdre's body. She was buried in a corner of a crowded city cemetery with no gravestone to mark the site. Her body would soon be lost among the mass of other bodies crammed into London's cemeteries.

After the burial, Charlotte and Betty led Kathleen away from the gravesite as quickly as they could. They could smell the bodies rotting under the muddy soil. All of London's terribly overcrowded cemeteries had become places to avoid because of the stench of decaying bodies. Charlotte thought about the peaceful green graveyard in which her infant son had been buried and the comfort she took from his tiny gravestone surrounded by plantings of ivy and laurel. She was grateful that she and Daniel had chosen to live in a new country instead of dirty, gloomy London where ordinary people could not afford even the slightest mark of human respect.

Kathleen could not go back to Ireland where the famine was growing worse with each passing day. She was grateful when Kumar Singh provided her with a railroad ticket and some pocket money so that she could go to her cousins in Liverpool. The struggle there would be just as difficult as the life she led in London, but at least she would have a few familiar people to help her make her way.

The fire damage in the Singh house was soon repaired, but Daniel made no headway trying to discover what had happened. The police showed no interest in the accident and refused to consider the possibility that the fire had been deliberately set.

"A lazy country slut set herself on fire and you expect the London Police Force to bother with that?" one of the police sergeants asked scornfully when Daniel went to the police station.

Kumar Singh had no more luck than Daniel did. There were very few of his countrymen in London and most English people were too suspicious of foreigners to care about helping them.

"If only we knew whether the peddler was an Englishman or a foreigner," Singh said to Daniel one day when they were sitting in a pub talking. "Who pays attention to peddlers?"

"That's it!" exclaimed Daniel. "Who would notice a peddler? It would have to be the women along your street. The cooks and kitchen maids keep an eye out for barrow men who are selling vegetables they might cook for dinner. We must question the servants in every home along the street."

"Do you mean that we should go from house to house asking questions of the servants?" asked Singh. "Would the householders ever allow such a thing?"

"You and I cannot do that. We cannot knock on kitchen doors and ask questions of the cooks, but perhaps a woman could. Mrs. Gallagher is very eager to find out what happened to her friend, Deirdre, perhaps she will be able to make enquiries."

When Daniel suggested the idea to Charlotte that evening, she seized upon the plan. "You know, I think I would be able to approach the kitchens along Mr. Singh's street. These last few days I have been deeply troubled about what would happen to my reading classes. I am afraid that even Betty will lose interest if her friends are no longer part of the group. I hope we can continue to meet at Mr. Singh's house, but Betty does not feel completely at home with the Indian women. I should try to find some other English, or Irish women to join us. There must be many other servants who are struggling to master reading and writing. I could use that as a pretext to talk with cooks and kitchen maids and learn more about what they know."

Daniel smiled at her eagerness. "Are you really intending to start a school for all the servants in London? Perhaps you will find so many eager students that you will outgrow the Singh's house."

"That is not likely. Servants work such long hours that few of them have enough interest or energy to take classes in the evening," Charlotte answered. "They have very little chance to change their lives, but I have every intention of teaching just as many willing students as I can. This would give me an opportunity to meet some of the people who live in this area and might want to learn. Perhaps it would make up a little for the teaching I was unable to do for Deirdre."

"I am sorry if I spoke lightly, Charlotte. It would be a lovely idea to start a class for some of the servants and working people here. People who haven't had a chance for an education. And if it helps us to discover any information about the man responsible for this horrible crime, that will be even better. There should be some punishment for whoever is responsible."

The next morning after Daniel had left for his office and Betty had trudged off to collect bundles of washing, Charlotte started her quest. The house directly next to the one where Kumar Singh lived was a well-kept building with tall, graceful windows on the first floor above the well-swept stone stoop. Down below on the ground floor, behind a small patch of brown earth dotted with scraggly bushes, the house had narrow, barred windows that let light into the kitchen area. In the quiet morning air, Charlotte could hear a woman's voice coming from the kitchen singing a familiar air:

In London town where I was born
There lived a fair maid dwellin'
Made every youth cry well away
And her name was Barbara Allen.

The singer had a light, sweet voice that floated out on the crisp air. Charlotte walked resolutely down the three steps to the area way and knocked briskly on the door. The voice stopped and soon the door opened. A young girl in a dark green dress with a stained white apron round her waist looked out in surprise.

"Oh, I thought you were the barrow man who brings the potatoes round each week. Who are you, Miss? Is it the cook you want to see?"

"May I come in for a minute? The air is chilly out here. I would like to talk with anyone who remembers the fire last week in the house next door. Do you remember that?"

"Indeed I do. We heard the screams of that poor young scullery maid that died." The girl shuddered and grimaced.

"Did you see anyone come by before the fire?" asked Charlotte. "Were there any peddlers stopping at the kitchen that morning? Anyone different from the peddlers or barrow men who you usually see?"

"Indeed I saw no one before I heard the sounds of that terrible fire. The cook sent me upstairs to carry a note to the mistress. She had an idea of something special she wanted to make for dinner and she sent the mistress a clipping from the newspaper. I read it myself and the cake sounded delicious, but then the commotion started next door and we all forgot about that."

Charlotte noticed that the girl could read. She was glad that some of the servants did. But she had to get on with her enquiries, so she asked whether the cook had seen anyone.

"You had better ask her yourself. Here she comes now from the market. And indeed the cook was soon there, bustling in with a basket of fish in her hand. She frowned when she saw a stranger in the kitchen, but when she heard Charlotte's question she was quick enough to answer.

"Oh, indeed that fire was something dreadful. We never had nothing like that happen before these strangers moved into the street. You know the man who lives in that house is as dark as the devil himself. And that cloth he wraps around his head! He's no Christian I warrant. My sister says it's as much as my life is worth to live in a city full of such strange, unchristian creatures. I've half a mind to move back to the nice quiet village where I grew up."

The woman seemed willing to talk on endlessly but Charlotte gently urged her back to the question of whether any peddlers or others had been around the neighborhood on the day of the fire.

"I'm not a woman who has time to waste staring out at the street, you know. But I do remember I saw a strange horse and wagon standing outside the door that morning. From the country it looked like, with a couple of barrels in back. Whether they were filled with potatoes or what I could not tell. Oh, and now that I think of it, the man who was driving the wagon was a dark complexioned man. He had his hat pulled down low on his face so I could hardly see what he looked like. And he weren't wearing anything strange on his head like that Indian next door, but he was almost as dark. Not a respectable man if you ask me. You wouldn't let a man like that into the kitchen, would you

Mary, if I were not here?" She glanced at the young kitchen maid who shook her head vigorously.

"Mary is a good country girl. She knows how to behave," the cook continued. "Not like those Irish next door. What with Indians and Irishmen running around the streets a real Englishwoman is not safe. I don't hold with letting foreigners into London. Let them stay where they belong and not bother decent folk with their fights and troubles."

"Did you happen to see whether that strange peddler went into Mr. Singh's kitchen?" asked Charlotte when the cook had finally stopped. "And after the fire started and there was a commotion in the house, was the peddler still on this street? Did either of you see his wagon leave? Someone must have seen him surely."

But the cook had no more to add to her story so Charlotte trudged on to the next house. She stopped at three other houses nearby but did not find a warm welcome. The servants she spoke to looked at her suspiciously and declared they had seen nothing strange on the street on the day of the fire. None of them invited her into their kitchen and she was unable to find out whether any of them might be interested in learning to read.

As usual the fog hung heavy over the city and the smoky air burned Charlotte's throat as she walked dejectedly back toward her lodging. Everyone on the street was hurrying along through the chilly weather. Most of them were wearing clothes not nearly warm enough to keep them comfortable. Perhaps that was why they looked so gloomy and unfriendly. At the busiest crossing on her way home, a small boy was helping women across the street, sweeping away sleety puddles from the pavement in front of their skirts, hoping for a ha'penny tip. His feet were bare and Charlotte's heart ached to think how cruelly they must hurt in the freezing rain. The poverty in London was appalling, far worse than in New York, and an air of hopeless suffering hung over the street.

On her way home, Charlotte stopped at the market to buy a piece of fish and a few small potatoes though the best she could find were wrinkled and looked old. By the time Daniel came home for his midday meal, she had cooked the meal and was ready for him, but she had no good news.

"Did you learn anything about the peddler?" Daniel looked at her expectantly.

"I found only one house where the servants would talk to me and I learned little enough there. The cook said she had glimpsed a dark-skinned peddler on the street, but then she began to harangue me with a story about the danger of foreigners in the city. I am not sure whether she saw a dark-skinned man or whether every stranger looks dark-skinned and threatening to her. You should have heard her going on about how his hat was pulled down low over his face and how respectable women like herself shouldn't be threatened with people who look different from them."

Charlotte sighed as she thought about the chattering cook. The woman had shown no sympathy for Deirdre and no interest in helping Charlotte. Was no one in the city paying attention? Did no one care?

"Even if there was a dark-skinned peddler on the street, or any kind of peddler, how could we find him again? The fire was started in Mr. Singh's house, so that must have been the target. Do you know anything about what enemies Mr. Singh might have?"

"Very little idea. You were here when he told us he had come to London to get back the jewel someone stole from his family. And he is seeking an audience with the Queen. If he is correct and if it is true that someone connected to the British government or to the East India Company is responsible for the loss, whoever is guilty of such a crime might want to silence him. Someone might be fearful that he will influence the Queen, but I am not sure that is likely. Even though he says he is an important man in India, and I am quite willing to believe him, I do not know that the Queen or her husband, Prince Albert, spend much time thinking about India. Surely they are more deeply concerned with problems closer to home."

"Yes," agreed Charlotte," with the Chartists holding demonstration and with the rebellious miners in the North, they scarcely have time to think about India And, of course, the Queen has young children to think about. The East India Company is only a commercial enterprise. Why would the Queen interfere with that?"

Charlotte had never thought much about England's colonies throughout the world. India was so far away from England. With so much poverty and suffering on the streets of London, why would the Queen care what was happening on the other side of the world?

"The British Army has been sent to protect the East India Company," Daniel reminded her. "All those soldiers are 'servants of the Queen' as they call themselves. There must be many families who have sons stationed in India and perhaps they have encountered natives, like Mr. Singh, and quarreled with them or even suffered at their hands."

"The chances of our finding the person responsible for the fire seem dim, don't they Daniel?" Charlotte was feeling gloomy again. "But I am not willing to give up. It makes me angry to think that people have forgotten Deirdre's death so quickly and dismiss it as an accident. That is not fair to her."

"I can meet with Mr. Singh again," said Daniel, "and see whether he can tell us more about his quarrels with the East India Company. Did he accuse someone of the theft of his family's jewel? He did not give us many details about that. Does someone have a grudge against him?"

"Yes, we should do that. And we need to learn more about other groups in the city who are likely to cause trouble. Wasn't there an article in your newspaper recently calling for the Queen to pay more attention to her subjects in England and not squander resources on foreign lands? Some people in the city, like the cook I spoke to, are angry at all the foreigners coming to London. Perhaps someone wants to injure Mr. Singh or at least drive him out of the country just because he is not English."

"Yes, Mr. Reynolds thinks that foreigners should go home. He feels very strongly that the Queen and her government have failed the workingmen of the country. In fact, he has declared that England should get rid of kings and queens and become a republic. A lot of the Chartists agree with him about that."

"We should find out more about the Chartists and whether they would be likely to attack Mr. Singh. Is the fire, and Deirdre's death connected with the death of Sean Costello? It seems strange that two such suspicious deaths should occur within a few days of each other."

CHAPTER ELEVEN

Casting a Net

After the others had left for work the next morning, Charlotte sat down at the kitchen table to write down her ideas. What should she do next to discover who caused the fire that killed Deirdre? When she and Daniel had first talked about living in London, she had looked forward to visiting a civilized city with wonderful historic buildings and beautiful homes. Most of the books she read all her life had come from London. She thought of it as a city filled with people in handsome drawing rooms reading books and talking about poetry.

Instead she had found a dreary, gloomy city filled with such poverty as she had never seen before. There had been beggars occasionally wandering along the roads in the village where she grew up, and a few on the streets of New York when she lived there, but this was different. In London, the streets were thronged with ragged people trying to make money by sweeping away the mud at street crossings or selling tiny bunches of flowers scavenged from the flower stalls. Charlotte had even seen a young boy carrying a tray with a large turtle on it and asking passers-by to pay to see it.

Charlotte had never seen the inside of a great house where people sat in comfort and read, but she saw rich men and women riding in carriages along the streets lined with poor people trying to make enough money to buy shoes. It was not surprising that city people growing up so close to the great houses and seeing how well the aristocrats lived should be filled with hatred for them and start thinking about a revolution. Tom and his friends on the docks would see the crates loaded with fancy furniture from France and pictures from Italy. All those costly items would grace the houses of the wealthy while the dock workers themselves lived on the streets or in hovels that could scarcely be called houses at all.

Poverty had come uncomfortably close to Charlotte in London. If she and Daniel had not become prosperous enough to afford comfortable lodgings, Tom and Betty might still be living on the street. And now Betty had whispered to her that she thought she might be with child. Where would they raise a child? Tom was a good hard worker, but there were hundreds of other men with backs just as strong as his who could unload ships and carry barrels. Unless he learned to read and got a trade, he would never have a life half as comfortable as the one she had built for herself.

With so much poverty around, there might be many people who would want to injure Kumar Singh. Seeing a dark-skinned man who lived a prosperous life could have increased the anger of people who hated the very idea of dark-skinned people coming to England. Was it an Englishman who had started the fire? The cook had told Charlotte that the peddler she had seen was dark-skinned himself. Was she right about that? Was he a real peddler? And if he was, how could she and Daniel possibly track him down? Whoever had caused the fire to flare up had thrown a chemical on it. That was an odd way to start a fire. Whoever was guilty must have known about ether. How many peddlers knew that? Perhaps the apothecary who sold the ether would remember the man who bought it. That was something Charlotte could start on.

Pulling on her cloak and putting on a bonnet, Charlotte prepared to brave the weather to find a nearby apothecary shop. She remembered seeing one on Tottenham Court Road, so she set off in that direction.

The shop was just as she had remembered it with a narrow doorway facing the street and two small, cloudy windows that allowed scarcely a glimpse of the inside. Above the door a discreet sign gave the name—Nathaniel Huntingdon, Apothecary.

As she drew near the shop, a man emerged and walked down the street away from her. He looked vaguely familiar and Charlotte frowned trying to remember who he might be, but he turned into a tailor's shop before she could identify him.

On entering the apothecary shop, Charlotte saw a dark wooden counter at the back, like the counter in a grocery shop. On shelves behind the counter were rows of flasks with labels. A marble pestle lay on the counter in front of a small, bearded man who presided over the store.

"Can I be of service to you, madam?" he asked Charlotte. "Do you require any pills today? Perhaps you or someone in your family is feeling poorly? Come closer. Do not be afraid. I have the most modern medicines to treat any illness."

"I am not looking for medicine, sir. I am enquiring about whether or not you sell ether, which I have heard is a remarkable compound for easing the pains of childbirth."

"Ah yes," the man answered peering at Charlotte suspiciously, "But if your sister or your friend requires such help, you had better find a doctor to help you. Are you a midwife?"

"No, no, I am not planning to assist a birth. I am asking because I have heard that such medicines are available and I want to find out whether I could buy some."

"Ether is a very strong drug. I do not sell such things to women. You had better send your husband here to purchase ether. It is too strong for women to handle."

"Ah, so you do sell them to men. I have a question for you. Has a dark-complexioned young man come in this past week to buy such supplies from you?"

"So you are not asking about childbirth? Surely you are not a participant in what the university men call 'ether frolics' in which they inhale the fumes of ether and enjoy the sensation? As I said, I would never sell such a drug to a woman."

"Indeed I am not interested in any frolics. I am trying to discover the cause of a fire nearby. I believe someone may have bought ether here and then accidentally started the fire."

"I do not sell a great deal of ether. The fire and death of that scullery maid was an accident. The police have told me so. It has nothing to do with me. It is true that one of my clients did buy quite a large amount of ether several days ago. He said he and his friends were going to have a frolic because some of them were leaving soon for India. There is no harm in that. He is a most respectable man. He paid cash readily enough and did not complain of the price. I warned him that ether was highly flammable and should be kept away from fire."

"Do you know where I could find this young man?" Charlotte asked eagerly, "Did you know his name?"

"No, I had no use for his name. I did not pay particular attention to him although I may have seen him about the neighborhood before. I do not pry into people's business, especially respectable people such as the ones I serve. The streets are filled with radicals and troublemakers. They are the people responsible for riots and unrest. Now, madam, if you do not wish to purchase anything today, perhaps I should get back to my work."

Charlotte thanked the apothecary for his time and turned toward the door. As she started walking slowly toward Cecil Court, she noticed a tall, erect man walking ahead of her—the same man she had seen earlier. When he turned his head to look into the small window of a bookshop, she caught a glimpse of his dark mustache. Then she realized it was Captain Granville, the army man she had seen at the Museum. The man who had spoken so scornfully of "heathen Indians". When he opened the door and went into the bookshop, she turned impulsively and followed him in.

Captain Granville strode toward the counter and started talking to the proprietor. Charlotte began to scan a shelf of books not quite sure what she was trying to find out. The bookstore was close to Mr. Singh's house, but that didn't mean it had any connection to the fire. She wondered whether Kumar Singh ever came to this bookstore to find books for his extensive library.

"Ah, Captain," she heard the proprietor say. "Are you looking for any more books about India and the Punjab? I am afraid I have nothing new in that line. There are some interesting volumes I have recently acquired concerning the troubles with radicals among the miners and other laborers. I believe you are interested in the radicals and what they are up to."

"Yes, I am interested. We have had many difficulties with those troublesome radicals.

Demanding a vote for every man. What nonsense! Universal suffrage would be the death of civilization. What does a coal miner know of the affairs of Parliament? Let me take a look at your new volumes."

The two men walked toward the back of the shop and leaned over a table to look at some books. Charlotte took the opportunity to slip out of the bookstore. What a lot of different opinions there were in London. Tom's friends wanted a vote for every man, while Granville and people like him thought that allowing poor men to vote would destroy the country. Each group was filled with angry men ready to fight for their beliefs. And what had this anger to do with Deirdre's death or with shootings outside the Palace? As she walked slowly back to their lodgings she thought about how impossible it would be to track down the men responsible for those crimes in a city the size of London.

Charlotte told Daniel about her visit to the apothecary as soon as he came home. She had already decided on their next step.

"Tom said last night that several of the men he works with on the docks have become radicals who want to make England a republic. We ought to get to know some of them. Both the apothecary and the bookseller talked about radicals as if they caused all the crime in the city. Can that be true? Perhaps these are the people we should be seeking to find the man responsible for the death of the policeman as well as the one responsible for the fire in Mr. Singh's house. Who was it that told Tom about this? Did he say the name was Jock something? Why don't we invite him here for a drink and something to eat after work? He might be able to tell us about the radicals."

"That's a good idea," Daniel agreed. "We can ask Tom if he will invite some of his friends over. We could have them over on Saturday. That should be a good day for them. Even Betty will be willing to leave her laundry work early. She deserves some rest to end the week."

Tom was enthusiastic about the plan, and so on Saturday when evening came he brought two of his friends, Jock and Walter, back to the house with him. They came into the house slowly, looking a little suspiciously at Daniel in business clothes, but they warmed up as the pints of beer came round. The man called Jock Fisher was a small, wiry man with broad muscular shoulders and arms, but rather spindly legs. His friend, Walter McGuire was larger and quieter. He had a lovely singing voice. Half an hour after they had arrived, they were singing their favorite song:

The time shall come when wrong shall end,
When peasant to peer no more shall bend;
When the lordly Few shall lose their sway,
And the Many no more their frown obey.
Toil, brothers, toil, till the work is done,
Till the struggle is o'er, and the Charter won!

The fire was warm, the eel stew Charlotte had made was delicious, and there was plenty of beer to wash it down with. Soon Jock and Walter were talking with Daniel and Charlotte like old friends. "It will be a pleasure to talk to a newspaper man about our ideas," Jock declared. "There's many a working man who would support the Charter if he knew more about it."

CHAPTER TWELVE

Life Stories

After they had all finished eating, Jock leaned back in his chair and started on his story.

"I was born and raised in the village of Byley like my father and grandfather before me. There's always been Fishers in Byley. My grandfather was a weaver and my father was brought up to the trade. There was a big loom standing in the cottage where I was born and I learned my colors from the wool almost before I could talk. In those days a weaver's trade was a good one and a family could live well. But that was before the machines came." He sighed and shook his head.

"Yes, I remember those days too," added Charlotte. "My father worked on farms around Bristol and there was food enough for all of us before the machines came. We grew potatoes and turnips and had some chickens we could slaughter for Sunday dinner. But that didn't last."

"No, the machines turned everything topsy-turvy," Jock agreed. "The men who could buy the machines built mills where they could weave the cloth at twice or three times the speed a weaver could do at home. They didn't need people who had served apprenticeships and learned the trade. What did they do? They hired the women and children out of the family.

"My mother and my two older sisters went into a mill and it nearly killed my father. It's a good thing my grandfather was dead by then. He would have been shamed to have his womenfolk working and him sitting at home minding the fire. My mother brought her pittance home from work and my father took it and went off to the pubs. We children were always hungry and before you know it we lost our cottage and the family broke up. My sister took up with a carpenter who travelled around building houses and looms and whatever was wanted. Annie, my sister, went off with him and we never heard no more of her. They might be up in Scotland or some such foreign place by this time."

"That's a terrible thing when a family breaks apart," Daniel agreed

All this time Jock's friend, Walter McGuire, had been sitting looking mournful as he listened to the story. Then he spoke up: "Same thing happened to my family. First my father left to look for work. He was a wool carder and good at his trade, but no one wanted him any more after the machines come in. He said he'd walk to Manchester to find work if he could, but we never knew whether he did or not. He left in early spring and he never did come back.

"No sense waiting for your father forever', says my mother and she finally took my sisters and me to Liverpool. We lived in such small, dark rooms we could scarcely move and my mother went out to be a washerwoman. At first she brought us back food every evening and we squeezed by, but then she met a man who worked at a pub and he wanted to marry her. Marry him she did and we moved into larger rooms, but my stepfather didn't like having children around. As my sister grew up, he bothered her so much she took to the streets to earn her keep. 'Might as well get paid for my body' she said 'and not give it away for free'. She soon learned to stay away all night and then she left and we heard no more from her.

"By this time I had two baby brothers and they were the only children my stepfather wanted around. As soon as I could get work on the docks I found places of my own to stay and didn't bother going back. I don't even know if my mother missed me."

Betty, who was listening open-mouthed to these stories, shuddered. "These cities are terrible places, ain't they? It's a wonder anyone lives here."

"But we'll put a stop to that, won't we Walter? And Tom, are you with us too?"

"How are you going to stop change?" asked Daniel. "Do you think the mill owners are going to shut down their machines? Do you think Parliament will change their minds and allow workers to organize unions?"

"They will when everyone gets a vote and the mill owners and aristocrats don't control Parliament," insisted Jock. "Our time is coming."

"Oh, Tom, will you be able to vote?" cried Betty. "And maybe I could vote too."

Tom laughed. "Women don't need to vote. You have a husband to vote for you. Didn't I promise to take care of you all your life?"

Charlotte had her doubts. "I know the Chartists want every man to have a vote. They want to abolish property requirements for Parliament too. It will never happen. Do you think the aristocrats will vote to let ordinary working people into Parliament?"

"I've seen those aristocrats," said Walter heatedly. "I've stood outside the Houses of Parliament and watched them get out of their carriages, wearing their fancy clothes and carrying their walking sticks. Half of them look too weak to walk a mile, much less to work for a living. Why should they rule over us?"

"They claim they inherit the right," agreed Jock, "just like they inherit their land and money, but times are changing. People are changing. You've heard of e-vo-lu-tion?" He almost spelled the word out. "I heard a lecture at our local hall last years that told us all about it. Creatures change. God didn't make some men to rule over others. Working men are getting stronger and smarter, they will take over the country. Those aristocrats are getting weak and womanish. It's science that tells us that."

Charlotte frowned in surprise. She had heard something about evolution in a lecture in Boston several years ago, but it was about animals and plants, not people. She looked at Daniel to see whether he knew anything about it.

"Are you a scientist?" Daniel was asking Jock. "I don't know much about this theory of evolution. It's a Frenchman who has written about it, isn't it? Man named Lamarck or something like that? Do you read French?"

"Not likely. But I understand a bit of it. My mother was a French woman. She came here after that revolution they had. She was a lady's maid and her mistress fled the country. She and her husband thought they could live in England just the way they had in Paris, but they didn't last long. The husband gambled away all his money and his wife's jewels too. Pretty soon they had to run away to Italy or someplace. They left all their servants behind. My mother ended up marrying my father while his business was still prosperous. She taught us all some French and my brother and I used to run out in the yard shouting 'Liberte! Equalite! Franternitie!'. But I never learned to read French."

The evening passed quickly with talking and a few songs. Charlotte and Daniel taught the Londoners the song they had learned from the Hutchinson Family Singers in New York.

The freedom train is coming,

Can't you hear the whistle blowing?
It's time to get your ticket and get on board
It's time for all the people to take this freedom ride
Get it together and work for freedom side by side.

They ended the evening singing a verse of *Auld Lang Syne* just as Charlotte remembered singing it at home when she was young. And then Jock and Walter went out into the foggy, smoky London air and walked home still singing.

Tom and Betty went to their room and Daniel and Charlotte companionably cleared up the remains of the food and put what was left in the pantry. "Do you think Jock is truly as radical as he sounds?" Charlotte asked. "Does he really think he and his friends can destroy the monarchy and have a republic? They have no army and the Queen has plenty of soldiers. For all the anger at that rally we went to, most British don't seem like rebels to me."

"No, England is a very law-abiding country. And Queen Victoria is nothing like the French king who was killed in their Revolution. It's not the Queen so much as the factory and mill owners that people are angry about. If Parliament would give more people the vote, I think most of the talk of rebellion would disappear."

An hour later, after Charlotte was asleep, she was suddenly awakened by a rattling noise. She sat up with a start. Where was it coming from? Then there was a louder sound and she realized someone was throwing stones at their door. By this time Daniel was awake. He went to the window and peered down at the street.

A flickering light from a lantern lit up a small space in front of their house, and when Daniel opened the window, they could hear scuffling. He yelled down at the man, but could not see anyone from the tiny window. "Get away, you rascal, before I come down and thrash you!"

Then he turned, pulled on his trousers, seized a candle and walked downstairs to confront the vandal. By the time he opened the door, whoever had been there was gone. There was no sign of anyone in the street, but when he looked at the door, Daniel could see words chalked on the door—"No more radicals. No more Charter."

The next morning Betty and Charlotte scrubbed the whitewashed words off the door. They wondered how many of their neighbors had seen the threatening language.

"Was it Jock and his friend they were after? What are they so angry about?" Betty worried.

Charlotte was worried too. She wondered how anyone could know that Walter and Jock had been there. Did someone follow Tom's friends? The thought of someone lurking around their house in the dark of night bothered Charlotte. She didn't want to admit to Daniel how disturbed she was by the idea of people watching them at home. Even the gray sky looked threatening.

CHAPTER THIRTEEN

Meetings and Strangers

On Monday morning Daniel was excited about the meeting he had arranged with Feargus O'Connor. Surely talking to one of the leaders of the Chartist movement would shed light on the reasons behind the attacks on the Queen. He had many questions about the tensions and anger that pervaded the city.

The two met in a dim tavern not far from the Houses of Parliament. O'Connor chose seats far toward the back of the tavern. "I don't want people seeing me meeting with a reporter," he said. "Because I am a radical and a supporter of the working man, many people would like to accuse me of being dangerous and wanting to overthrow society."

"For several years now you have been trying to make working people more prosperous and to extend the vote. You surely have many more supporters than enemies among the common people."

"Aye, there's many people who support O'Connor. Indeed there are. There are those who call me the 'Lion of Freedom' and think of me as their champion. But there are others who deliberately cause trouble at our demonstrations and try to turn us into villains."

"Who are these people? What are they trying to do?" Daniel wanted to get the names of O'Connor's enemies.

"I don't know all of their names, although some people are openly hostile. But I know there are secret troublemakers who attend our demonstrations just to cause trouble and turn people toward violence. They commit crimes and send about the word that it is the Chartists and radicals who are to blame. That young policeman, Sean Costello, was killed and now people are saying it was a madman—a man driven mad by radical ideas who killed him. I don't believe it for a minute. That was a conspiracy by people who want to see more radicals thrown into prison."

"What are they afraid of? Who are they?" Daniel asked urgently. "Do you have any names? Of course the great land owners who control Parliament now do not want working men to vote. The manufacturers who can hire men and women to work in their factories without paying a decent salary want the radicals put down. Can you imagine what will happen to them when every man has a vote? The law will insist that workers are paid fair wages."

"That's it, you see. We're at the dawn of a new era of progress. Those who have money themselves are hoping to keep it all and raise more. But people are beginning to learn that they don't have to sell their labor to anyone at whatever price. As the poet says:

Men of England wherefore plough
For the lords who lay ye low?
Wherefore weave with toil and care
The rich robes your tyrants wear?

People understand now that they can take power for themselves as long as they unite and fight for the Charter. There's many an aristocrat who is frightened and will do anything to keep the common people down. You mark my words, young man, the struggle will get worse before it gets better."

O'Connor had scarcely finished speaking when a tall figure loomed up beside their table. The man who smiled down at them was dressed in the red jacket of an Army man and carried himself with a military swagger.

"Sit down! Sit down! And have a pint with us," O'Connor invited jovially as he turned to Daniel to introduce him. "This is Sargent Donegan of the 67th Regiment of Foot. They should be off fighting the heathen in India, but here he is in London."

"A man gets tired of fighting the heathen sometimes," said Donegan as he sat down. "We took them on in the Punjab and now we're enjoying a bit of a rest. It was a grand fight though we lost a good many men. Those savages would rather cut down a man from behind than have a fair fight like civilized people."

"Well, they're fighting for their country," Daniel interjected. "You can't blame them too much for wanting to keep the British army out. There's many an Irishman wants to keep the English Army away."

"You cannot compare Indians to the Irish," sputtered Donegan. "Indians are heathen with peculiar habits and peculiar gods. They keep their women locked away and when a man dies his widow has to throw herself on the funeral fire and die too. Did you ever hear of anything so cruel? Would you want your mother to throw herself on your father's funeral pyre? It's not human to be so cruel. The Indians are lucky the English will bother with them. We are civilizing them."

Daniel remained silent in the face of such passion.

"The English are making them Christians and teaching them how to behave themselves," Donegan insisted. "Besides, they are making us rich," he added with a chuckle. "You should see the gold and jewels they have hidden away. After we won a few battles, the General took home a fortune and every soldier in the regiment got some prize money to take home."

He took another long pull on his pint and leaned across the table to whisper in a hoarse voice, "Besides the prize money, there are jewels and gold lying around in those palaces just begging to be picked up. Why should those heathens have such baubles? We're bringing civilization to India so it's only right that we should get some reward. Well, I'm off, gentlemen." He swallowed the last of his pint. "There's more to see in

London than the inside of a smoky pub. I'll be enjoying myself for a while before it's my turn to ship out again."

When Daniel went back to his newspaper office he continued thinking about political matters and foreign people. He was looking again at the newspaper and reading his article about Kumar Singh, which had just been published. Daniel had tried to explain Kumar's feelings about the East India Company in the Punjab and the actions that had caused so much bad feeling. Mr. Reynolds had praised the article and Daniel felt proud of his work.

His pleasant thoughts were interrupted by a loud knock on the office door. When Daniel answered it, he saw the officer who had been at the Museum reception.

"I am Captain Granville, sir," the man sounded angry as he spoke. "I would like to question the person who wrote the article in this newspaper about the Punjab."

"I am responsible for that article," Daniel replied. "My name is Daniel Gallagher and I believe we have met before—at the British Museum."

"Ah yes, I remember you. Very interested in Indian jewelry and trinkets are you not? You seem extremely fond of heathens and their habits. This article you have written is an insult to British soldiers and all the men who represent our country in foreign lands."

"I beg to differ. It is no insult to discuss the beliefs and complaints of people who live in some of the far-flung countries where the British do business. Tell me what you think is insulting about the article. Please sit down. I am eager to hear your thoughts."

The captain looked rather surprised when Daniel said that, but he sat down, still grasping his walking stick in one hand.

"We English have brought Christianity to India. We have introduced Hindus and other heathen to the Bible and cured them of some of their evil habits. But have they thanked us? No. They flaunt their wealth and show us their idols and expect us to think they are just as good as we are."

"But many of them are honorable men," Daniel protested. "As my article showed, Kumar Singh was treated contemptuously by British soldiers and Company officials because he is not considered their equal. Many responsible men, some of them members of government, would agree that this is not fair. They have spoken out about the excesses of some of the British forces in India. You can scarcely blame the Sikhs and other Indians for wanting to be respected in their own territory where their people have been living for generations."

"Let them stay in their godforsaken territory with their gold and jewels and heathen idols, but they must accept the direction and care of a superior, civilized country. The only Englishmen who object to our behavior in India are the radicals who want to weaken our country. Indeed some of them have even attacked our Queen. Are you one of them, Mr. Gallagher?"

"I am not a radical," protested Daniel. "But some of their ideas are worth our attention. In this newspaper we strive to give our readers the ideas that are being circulated among men of influence in this city."

The Captain did not seem inclined to argue further about ideas. He leaned over Daniel's desk and frowned menacingly, "Well, sir, I shall remember what you have said. My friends and I will be watching this newspaper. If you step over the boundaries and criticize our Queen and country too much, you will take the consequences."

With that, he left the room and clattered down the stairs, his back ramrod stiff. Daniel turned again to his article about Kumar Singh and the actions in the Punjab region of India where the Sikhs lived. At Kumar's request he had written nothing about the theft of the emerald, but only about the way the East India Company and the British Army were treating the native rulers in the region.

Daniel went home soon after Captain Granville left the office. Over dinner he and Charlotte talked about the anger Daniel's article had caused. When Tom joined them, fairly early in the evening, he had to hear the story all over again.

"I'm not surprised," said Tom. "People are angry about everything. Two men on the docks got into a fight this afternoon about whether all the men who have been moving here from the countryside these days should be allowed to take jobs away from Londoners. It got so bad the foreman sent everyone home except for a couple of men who were unloading the last ship in from India. I lost hours of pay because of that fight. That makes me angry."

While Tom and Daniel talked at home, work at the docks continued.

Walter and Jock were among the handful of men still unloading cargo from a ship called *Nemesis*. After all the large crates had been removed, the crew tossed smaller personal trunks down to the workmen as fast as they handle them. Light was fading from the sky and most of the dock workers had left and were scattering to their homes when one of the trunks tumbled into the shadows several yards away from the main unloading area. Walter knelt down on the stone paving and pulled up the top of the small trunk. The fall had caused the lock to pop open and contents of the over-full trunk were spilling out. Walter gasped as he saw that several revolvers had fallen to the ground. Quickly he and Jock threw the mysterious weapons back into the trunk, and pulled it over to the shelter of a warehouse next to the quayside. They knew they had only a few minutes to work before whoever was picking up the trunk would come to get it.

The revolvers glinted in the light from the sinking sun. Walter stared at them covetously. If only he had one of those, he could inspire his friends to help him make changes all right. Suddenly he had a plan. He grabbed a loose piece of cloth that had been wrapped around the guns, tore it in half and improvised a sling for his arm as though he were injured.

"What the devil are you doing?" Jock muttered.

"Slip one of the revolvers in here. Quick! Quick! We don't have much time. We can use a gun better than whatever fancy gentleman owns the trunk."

Almost as soon as he had said that, the gentleman himself appeared, his walking stick clamped under his arm, and pushing a handcart. "You two," he called. "You'll have a shilling if you put the trunk on this cart and push it around to my place."

"Oh, aye, sir, we'll do that," Walter said. "My arm is sore but with two of us it'll be no trouble at all."

"Just follow me this way. It's only around the corner and past those shops over there." The man directed them. "Do you men work on the docks regularly? What are your names? I might have jobs for a couple of strong young fellows like you."

"My name is Walter McGuire, and that's my friend Jock Fisher. There's lots of jobs we could do for a gentleman like you."

"Here we are. This is my lodging. He opened the door and gestured them toward a doorway on the ground floor. "Just leave the trunk at the door here. I've a shilling in my pocket, but I've a bit more business with ye."

The man turned to Walter suddenly and grabbed at the sling on his arm, pulling it open so the revolver clattered to the floor. Walter pulled back quickly and struck out with his other arm. "What you doing? I ain't done nothing wrong."

Jock turned toward the street door but realized the way was blocked by the man who had hired them and who now loomed over them with his walking stick raised threateningly.

"Do you think I'm blind that I didn't see you had one of my guns tucked into that bandage of yours? I could drag the two of you down to the police court right now and tell them I've caught a pair of thieves. Who do you think they'd believe—a respectable Captain who serves the Queen or a pair of ruffians from the quayside?"

Jock and Walter recognized the truth of what he was saying and stood silently glaring at him.

"But I'm no great admirer of the police myself," the Captain continued, "and as I said, I might have a couple of jobs for you. I'll pay you fair enough, but if you ever breathe a word about anything you do for me, I'll tell the police you're a pair of thieves that stole my revolver and you'll soon regret your flapping tongues."

It didn't take long for Jock and Walter to agree that doing a few jobs for the Captain would be fine with them.

"I'll know how to find you then. If you get a message down on the docks that Captain Saxon wants you for something, you can come up here to my lodging and meet me. If you're trusty men and hard workers I might even give you one of these revolvers someday."

CHAPTER FOURTEEN

The Second Class

On Thursday, Charlotte returned to the Singh's house to hold another class. The rain was pelting down so hard Betty could not go to pick up her loads of washing. Nothing would dry in this cruel rain, she said, so she quickly agreed to go with Charlotte and join the class of Indian women for a reading lesson

They splashed their way through the muddy street. Most of the peddlers had stayed home today, even the market women huddled under the makeshift canvas roofs of the market stalls, were having difficulty keeping their goods from being washed away. Charlotte wondered whether some of the Indian women would stay away from class because of the weather.

When they arrived at the Singh's house, however, they found the same six women perched on the chairs at the long table. Charlotte had underestimated the strength of their desire to learn to read. They had all braved the rain and not only had they arrived at class but they had remembered the letters they learned the last time they were there. They were even more quiet

135

and subdued than they had seemed the first day she met them.

Charlotte noticed that all of the women had pulled their scarves close around their heads and one of them kept glancing over her shoulder as though she suspected danger was lurking somewhere in the house. Charlotte hoped she would be able to keep their minds on her lesson and not let the students worry too much about Deirdre, but her presence hovered over the room. Perhaps it would be best to speak about her openly.

"You all know we have lost one of our friends who used to be in this class. Perhaps today you would like to practice writing a sentence of sorrow for Deirdre."

Betty was the first to speak. "'Rest in peace, Deirdre'. That's what the vicar says at funerals. I will write that down."

"She has gone from the darkness into light," another woman said. "Can you help me write that? That is what my maharani would say about someone who died."

"What is a maharani?" asked Betty curiously.

"The woman I work for is a maharani. Her husband was the ruler of a kingdom in in India. That is why she is now a maharani."

"Oh yes," Meena chimed in. "I know your maharani. She was a friend of my mother, and she has been my friend too. I called upon her when we first came to London and she helped me to understand how to live in a British house. She has been many times in

London. When she comes back to London again I hope to see her often. She is traveling in Europe now."

Charlotte was pleased that her pupils were able to overcome some of their sorrow as they wrote and read their tributes to Deirdre. Soon the talk moved to questions about colors in the saris that the maharani and other women wore. Knowing the names of all the colors in English and being able to read them easily would be useful for all of these women.

"I practiced my alphabet by writing letters in some flour that cook spilled on the table," said one woman. "And for the first time the cook looked at me with respect." She smiled shyly and pulled her red-flowered sari closer around her face.

"And I was able to write my name for the young master," boasted another. "He is only a child but he has always thought he was smarter than I am. Now I can write my name 'Dalaja' and he thinks I have become a wise women."

"Let's sing a song for Deirdre," suggested Charlotte. "Do any of you know songs?"

The women looked at one another without saying anything. Finally the one called Dalaja spoke up. "I can sing a song my mother taught me, but it is an Urdu song. You will not understand the words."

She sang a soft, crooning song that Charlotte decided must have been an Indian lullaby. The melody sounded somewhat monotonous to Charlotte, but all of the women recognized it and smiled and sang along. It clearly brought them great pleasure.

"Do you know any songs in English?" Charlotte asked.

"Well, there is one that the young master sings sometimes. He sings it very loudly while he is playing with his tin soldiers. I have heard it so many times that I can remember the words.

Rule Britannia!
Britannia rule the waves
Britons never, never, never shall be slaves.

Meena Kaur frowned and interrupted the song. "Stop that!" she cried out, "We will not sing songs about Britain ruling everyone. That is what they want to do. They want to rule all of India from the Punjab to the Tamil country. I will never sing a song about their ruling the world. And you must leave this class, Dalaja."

"Oh, I am so sorry," Charlotte tried to explain. "I did not think about what the words meant. I am sure that Dalaja did not mean any harm. She was only singing a childish song she had heard a little boy sing. Come, let's forget about that. I will teach you an American song that our soldiers sang when they were breaking away from England. It has a very funny name, "Yankee Doodle Dandy".

Yankee Doodle went to town

A-riding on a pony,
Stuck a feather in his cap
And called it macaroni.

Yankee Doodle keep it up,
Yankee Doodle dandy,
Mind the music and the step,
And with the girls be handy.

All the women enjoyed that song and they sang it several times before going back to the difficult task of copying their letters onto their slates. Meena Kaur seemed to forget her anger, but Charlotte wondered how strongly she felt about the British rule in India. Daniel had told her how Kumar Singh had talked about his experiences with the East India Company, but his wife looked so young, almost childlike, that Charlotte had not expected she would have strong feelings about political matters.

CHAPTER FIFTEEN

Danger in the Afternoon

After Charlotte's class had left the house, Meena Singh retreated to the parlor where she looked at some of the books Charlotte had left behind for her. Even after only two class sessions, London was beginning to feel more friendly. The women in Charlotte's classes were all serving girls and not at all like Meena's own sisters and cousins, but at least they spoke the same language and knew what the Indian sun felt like

Only one thing troubled her, so she turned to Parni, "Had you ever heard that song before? The one about Britannia?"

Parni shook her head mutely. The only songs she had ever heard were the ones sung in Meena's household.

"It was a horrid song. I know my husband would never allow such a song in his house. It was wrong of Mrs. Gallagher to let Dalaja sing it. Well, I guess she couldn't know what happened. What does she know of India after all?"

They sat comfortably in the parlor for some time and then Kumar Singh's manservant, Rahil, came to tell them that an Indian woman was outside asking to see Meena.

"But who could she be?" Rahil had no answer.

Meena hesitated, knowing that in her father's house she would never receive anyone who had not been vouched for by her husband. But this was England and she was beginning to think she should take some of the liberties that English women had. She clapped her hands imperiously.

"Show her in," she instructed Rahil.

The woman who appeared was far older than Meena had expected. She was dressed in a simple white sari and walked slowly as though she were a very, very old woman. Parni jumped up and led the woman into the room. "Sit here, grandmother," she said respectfully. "Let me get you a soft cushion for this chair."

"Thank you, my child," said the woman speaking English in a soft voice. They had to strain to hear her. "My mistress, Maharani Ahuja Kaur, has been a good friend to your family in Amritsar and she has news of them to share with you. She has recently returned to London, but suffers from the chilly weather She has sent me to invite you to have tea with her. She will only be here for a short time. She sails on one of the great ships in the morning. But she has sent her carriage to bring you to her at the hotel where she is staying."

Parni ran to the window and pulled back the heavy curtains. She gestured to Meena who joined her. Sure enough an elegant carriage was standing at the door. Meena hesitated but then she thought of Charlotte who walked around the streets of London freely, going wherever she wanted to go. Even the Indian servant girls seemed to have no fear. Surely she, daughter of a mighty Raja, could be as brave as they.

"We will go with you," she said to the old woman. Parni brought warm wraps for both the women and Rahil opened the door for them, looking rather worried. They walked with their sari-clad visitor to the waiting carriage. When the woman opened the door, Meena could see a figure in dark clothes sitting on one of the benches. She hesitated a moment, but the Maharani's serving woman urged her and Parni to go inside the closed carriage and then climbed in after them. They could hear the coachman snap his whip and the carriage started to roll down the street.

Meena looked at the man who sat on the carriage seat opposite her and Parni. He was wearing English clothes, with a scarf wound tightly around his neck and covering most of his chin. He did not remove his hat when the women entered, which startled Meena. She began to chatter nervously in English.

"I have never been in a carriage with a man before. This must be the day when I start acting like an Englishwoman. My mother would be surprised to see me and I am afraid my father would be angry. Perhaps my husband will be angry too."

She paused, but there was no answer. The man did not say a word and neither did the old woman who had brought them to the carriage. Meena felt Parni shrinking closer into her as though she wanted protection. Surely there could be nothing to fear. These people knew her family. The carriage started to move faster and Meena turned to the window and tried to draw back the curtain.

"Don't do that, Madam," spoke up the silent Englishman. "Let the curtain remain. You have no need to look outside. It is a cold winter day."

The carriage lurched to one side as it turned a sharp corner. The sound of the wheels changed as though they were rolling over very rutted paving stones. Meena became angry. "I certainly can look out the window if I wish," she said imperiously in the same positive voice she had used at home for the boys who swept the yard. She reached toward the curtain again but the old woman caught her hand and pulled it back.

"You are not the ruler here, Missy," she said. Her voice was louder now and did not sound like a woman's voice. The sari slipped from her head and Meena realized with horror that the old woman was really a man, and not a very old man either. He had been stooped and looked frail when he was in their house, but now he raised his head, leaned against the cushion and smiled grimly at her.

"We fooled you all right, didn't we?" he said smugly. "I am quite an actor. You were completely taken in. Did you really think the Maharani might be in London? I am afraid she is miles away. She is probably in Amritsar, perhaps taking tea with your family right now."

"Where are you taking us? My husband will see that you are punished for this."

"First he has to find us, doesn't he. Don't worry. We will take good care of you and your maid. We will not hurt you. You are far too precious. Your husband will give us what we want to get you back safely. You have nothing to fear as long as he is sensible and agrees to our terms quickly."

Meena's heart was beating so rapidly it hurt her chest. She strained to hear what was going on outside and tried to guess where they might be. But she knew almost nothing of London. All those days of staying at home had not taught her anything about the city. She might was well be in Zanzibar as in this unknown English city. How would her husband ever find her?

The horses slowed down and stopped. Meena heard a metallic sound as iron gates shut behind them. The man who had visited them in disguise ushered them out of the carriage. Night was falling fast and Meena could scarcely see, but she knew they were standing in the courtyard of a large gray building. Tall stone walls surrounded the yard so there was no glimpse of anything outside except for a small far-off moon shining fitfully through streaks of cloud.

CHAPTER SIXTEEN

Missing

When Kumar Singh returned home later that day, he was astonished to discover his wife was not there. Rahil explained about the visit from the Maharani's servant, but Kumar was uneasy

"This servant expected my wife to go with her into a strange carriage and drive across the city alone with her?"

"Your wife took young Parni with her. She said that she was in London and could act like a British woman now. She was very firm, sir." Rahil twisted his hands together and bent his head as he stood before Kumar. "She is the mistress of this house."

"Yes, yes, indeed she is," admitted Kumar. "But this is very strange and it makes me uneasy. They have been away too long and have sent no word. I will make inquiries." He made up his mind to ask the Gallaghers whether they had any idea of what had happened, so he marched over to their house and knocked loudly.

Daniel opened the door and saw Kumar Singh, his magnificent turban damp with rain, standing outside.

When he came in, he said urgently: "They have taken my wife away! Do you know anything about this? Is Mrs. Gallagher here? Something must be done immediately."

"Have you notified the police?"

"What have the police to do with it? This is my wife. She is my concern and I will take care of her myself without the British police. But I must find out where she is." His voice rose with an anguished tone.

Meanwhile Charlotte had come to stand behind Daniel. "Meena Kaur was fine when I left her late this afternoon. That was not very long ago. What could have happened?"

Daniel ushered Mr. Singh into the parlor and more details came out. "My servant Rahil admitted a caller, an elderly woman who did not have a card but wanted urgently to see my wife. The woman was dressed in a white sari, but she spoke English. My wife insisted on seeing her and after a short conversation, she and her young serving girl left with the woman. They drove away in a handsome carriage. Rahil said it looked like a maharani's carriage."

"Did they tell Rahil where they were going or when to expect them back?"

"No. Rahil was uneasy, but my wife is a very young woman and she can sometimes be headstrong. Oh, why did I not stay at home yesterday instead of paying fruitless calls on government officials? I would never have allowed this to happen." Kumar Singh frowned and clenched his fists.

"Did Rahil overhear anything of what they said?"

"He thought he heard my wife say something about the maharani returning to Amritsar tomorrow. That could only be the Maharani Ahuja Kaur, who has been a friend of my wife's family for many years. I have not heard that she is in London and am surprised that she would not have called upon my wife or written to let us know she was in the city."

"We must try to find this maharani, if it is indeed she, and find out what has happened," Daniel declared. "Perhaps we will discover there is nothing to worry about. If she were in London, where do you think she would be staying?"

"There are some hotels and guesthouses in this city where certain Indian travellers are made welcome when their business brings them to London. And there are a few Indian families living in the city who have welcomed me and my wife to London. We can visit the Maharani's London residence, although I do not believe she is in the city at this time. She visits London only occasionally when she wishes to buy English goods."

The two men left the house to investigate the possibility that Meena Kaur might be visiting the Maharani at her residence. Charlotte, Betty and Tom waited for them impatiently.

"There's been foul play," Tom said firmly. "Why would this old woman suddenly appear and take the women away? There have been too many odd things going on in this city lately if you ask me."

In little more than half an hour Kumar Singh and Daniel had returned. Their downcast faces told the story of their failed quest. Kumar spoke.

"The housekeeper at the Maharani's residence told us that her mistress was not expected back from her trip to Europe until later in the year. She assured us that no servant had been sent to invite my wife to visit her. No guests were expected at the house until the Maharani and her staff returned. Neither the housekeeper nor the butler there knew anything about this."

The hour was late, so Kumar Singh reluctantly went home hoping there would be some word waiting for him to tell him what had happened to his wife. The others talked a bit longer.

"Do you suppose someone kidnapped Meena?" Betty asked the question they had all been reluctant to raise.

"Why would anyone do that?" Charlotte responded. "What would they gain? Do you think Kumar Singh has enough money to pay a large ransom?"

"Perhaps it is not money they are after," Daniel added. "Perhaps they believe they can gain something from him. What would he have to offer them?"

"Maybe they just hate these foreigners coming into the country. Maybe they want to scare the Singhs so they go away and never come back," suggested Tom. "Some of my mates at the docks would be just as glad to see all those darkies disappear."

"Even the cook at the Singh house talked about dark-skinned people who were coming into the country," Charlotte added. "Even though she worked for the Singhs, she didn't seem fond of them. She didn't even have just the loyalty you would expect any cook to have for her employers."

"The cook and the kitchen maid," exclaimed Daniel. "We should ask them whether they saw the old woman who came to the house. I wonder how much they talk about the Singhs when they meet with their friends on their days off."

"The cook might gossip, but she wouldn't know about the maharani, would she?" Charlotte asked. "Perhaps Mr. Singh's servant Rahil is the one who has talked."

There were too many questions and too few answers to deal with that evening. The next day after the others had gone off to work, Charlotte decided she would return to the Singh's house and ask the cook and kitchen maid whether they had seen anything suspicious. She was afraid they might not talk freely with her because they probably had seen her teaching at the house before. But it would not hurt to try.

Now that spring was coming, the weather was a little warmer. The daylight came earlier and lingered later, cheering Charlotte considerably. The London sky was still darkened by smoke and soot, but fresh spring winds made it a bit easier to breathe. Charlotte walked briskly along the now-familiar streets to the Singh's house. Once there, she went downstairs to the area and knocked on the kitchen door.

The kitchen maid opened the door and looked surprised. "Oh, it's you again. You have been here before to ask about that peddler. Not much news we could give you about that. But this is an unlucky house. The fire was bad enough, but now the mistress has left and the master is looking very sorrowful."

"Who's there?" shouted a voice from inside the kitchen. "Don't stand gossiping, Mary. We have work to do."

"May I speak to the cook?" asked Charlotte entering the kitchen.

The cook was standing at the kitchen table deboning a large fish with skillful hands. She recognized Charlotte immediately. "You are the young women was asking about the peddler a while ago. And now you have more questions, do you? You are friends with the mistress now, I know. I seen you walk up to the front door and knock, bold as brass."

"Yes, I am a teacher and Mrs. Singh arranged for me to teach a group of servant girls that she knows. Many of these girls can't read, you know, so they will never be able to become a cook as you are. You must read many cookery books and recipes."

"Aye, that I do. I had a good education in the village school. Nothing fancy, mind you, but we learned to read our Bible and the newspaper too. I was able to sign my name in the register when I married, though there's many who can't. And now my poor husband's gone to his grave, I can write a letter to his mother to comfort her in her old age. But what these young Indians want with reading and writing I don't know. They will never be cooks here. They don't know the proper English dishes. It's strange food they want to eat. The master eats like an English gentleman, I'll say that for him, but the mistress makes such a face sometimes I know she longs for the greasy Indian food she's used to."

Once again Charlotte had to wait patiently hoping the cook couldn't talk forever. Finally she had a chance to break in, "When did you last see your mistress?"

"Yesterday at dinner. She weren't here for the evening meal and the master never ate his neither. He was so worried about her. She went out and never came back."

"Did you see her leave? Do you know who she went with?"

"I caught just a glimpse of them—the mistress and young Parni and a strange-looking woman wrapped up in a white shawl. . She was a strong woman, I'll say that, even though she was old. Practically lifted the mistress up into the carriage like a man would."

"Did you hear them say where they were going?"

"Heard nothing at all, but they seemed like they were in a hurry to go. They whipped right off down the street. What are you so curious about the mistress for? She's a little thing. Never says hardly a word to me and has no sense about giving orders for the household. The master has to do that. But everyone is curious about the mistress."

"Who else has been curious about her?"

"Oh, the delivery man who came with the coal last week. Asked whether this was the house where the foreign lady in the strange, pretty dresses lived. Wanted to know who she was and why she and her husband were here."

"Did he say why he was so curious about them? Did he know them?"

"He didn't know much about them. I told him they was important people who know royalty in India. The master goes to the Palace, you know, and sometimes he gets mail from there. That Rahil of his tells us he knows half the royalty in India. They are very important people."

"So you told the coal delivery man about the important people Mr. Singh knows?" Charlotte was beginning to understand why someone might want to kidnap Meena Singh in the hope of getting ransom from her husband.

As she walked back home, Charlotte pondered what she had learned. It seemed possible that someone was plotting against Kumar Singh. Did they think he was a very wealthy man who would pay a handsome ransom, or was there some other reason he had been targeted? And no matter what the reason—was Meena Kaur all right? Was she in danger?

CHAPTER SEVENTEEN

Searching for Meena

Charlotte could not shake off thoughts of the two terrible things that had happened since she and Daniel arrived in London. Deirdre's death in a fire was unbelievably tragic. The vision of her suffering haunted Charlotte's dreams. And now Meena's disappearance. Meena was so young and had led such a sheltered life. She would be totally unprepared for harsh treatment. Charlotte's stomach tightened in pain as she thought of what might happen.

Daniel had promised to ask the writers and editors at the newspaper what they might know about feuds among the Sikhs and other Indians who lived in London. Perhaps the men who took Mrs. Singh were enemies of Kumar Singh from India. Perhaps they had brought their quarrels with them to England.

Who else might be trying to cause trouble? Charlotte remembered the words scrawled on their door the evening that Walter and Jock had called on them. "Kill the radicals!" They had never found out who had done that. Walter and Jock were certainly radicals. But foreigners were feared and disliked too. Many people who hated and feared radicals also scorned foreigners. Was Kumar Singh the target of this kind of feeling? Daniel worked for a radical newspaper; perhaps he was also hated. So far no one had tried to harm Charlotte— it was Meena Singh they had taken. With so much unrest and so many strong feelings among different groups of people, how could she possibly find out who was responsible for this particular crime?

The only person she knew who spent time with radicals—men who talked about causing trouble and fighting for their rights—was her brother Tom. Charlotte turned her steps toward the docks where he and his friends worked. As she wormed her way through the crowd of barrow men and the women selling coffee and pastries, she wondered how they felt about foreigners like the Singhs. The Chartists were struggling for the rights of Englishmen. Did they think immigrants and other foreigners threatened those rights?

She stopped to buy hot coffee from a gnarled old woman in a dress so faded there was no color left in it except a washed out gray. And the blanket shawl over her shoulders, which might once have been red, was faded to a dusky pinkish plaid. The woman smiled at Charlotte, exposing the three or four blackened teeth in her mouth.

"How are you, dearie? I have some lovely pastries. Would you like a piece? Only a ha'penny each." She held out a thin and claw-like hand and Charlotte gave her a coin and took the pastry. The sweet looked old and tasted stale, but the woman chuckled and kept calling out her wares. "Fresh pastries, ha'penny each! Come get your fresh pastries."

The day, which had started out sunny, was turning gray and raindrops started spattering down on the street. When Charlotte saw St. Barnabas Church, she decided to stop in until the shower was over. She was getting nowhere with her search and probably wouldn't be able to find Tom anyway. Maybe it was a silly notion to go to the docks to look for him. She made her way toward the church and climbed the steps. Two old women were sitting in the shelter of the doorway begging for coins from passers-by.

Charlotte made her way into the church and sat down in a pew near the back. The church was gloomy, lightened only by the greenish light coming in through dull, ancient glass windows. A few figures were moving around or kneeling in front of the altar. Charlotte was startled when she saw a knot of three or four men clustered in one of the pews talking softly among themselves. One got up to leave and Charlotte recognized Tom.

As he walked toward the door of the church, Charlotte rose and followed him outside. He moved quickly away from the church and Charlotte had to almost run to catch up with him.

"Tom, Tom what were you doing in the church?"

"Where did you come from? I was just talking to some of the men I work with. We sometimes come here for a quiet talk when we can rest from the unloading. It's not safe to talk in a pub where anyone might overhear."

"What are you talking about that is so dangerous you don't want anyone to overhear you? They are not plotting an uprising are they? You'd better stay away from them if they are. You don't want to get into more trouble with the police."

Tom's eyes evaded Charlotte's. He mumbled something about, "Women don't understand. We must stand up for our rights. We must..." His voice dwindled away as Charlotte looked at him sternly.

"I know you want to do what's right, Tom, but you have responsibilities now. You must take care of Betty. What would happen to her if you went to prison or were hurt? Daniel and I won't be able to care for her forever. And there are dangerous people in this city."

As she walked with him toward the quays, ignoring the raindrops that were beginning to soak through her shawl, Charlotte scolded him like the big sister she was. "Kumar Singh has been trying to change things— to influence the Queen and make the government more respectful of Sikhs—and now his wife has been kidnapped. What does that mean? This is a dangerous world. Tell me what you and your friends are planning."

"I have to get back to work," Tom insisted. "I'll tell you more when I get home tonight." He darted off so quickly that Charlotte had no chance to ask anything else. She turned back toward the church. She would try to dry off a bit before heading for home. London showers came and went so quickly that she wouldn't need shelter for long.

The church was almost empty now, although the two begging women still huddled in the doorway and a few other people clustered in the pews near the entrance waiting for the shower to be over. Charlotte walked slowly around the walls of the church trying to think what the next step should be in trying to find Meena Kaur. She did not know any of the Sikh families in the city, so Kumar Singh would have to find and question them. Another thought struck Charlotte. Was Meena kidnapped because she was a foreigner, or was it only because some people thought her husband was wealthy and would pay a good ransom?

Charlotte sat down in a pew near the center of the church. She glanced around at the tall windows and the gray walls, dank with the damp of a London winter. A sign with archaic printing was on the wall next to her "Entrance to crypt. Key with sexton." Who would want to go down into the crypt, she wondered, perhaps family members keeping an eye on their long-dead ancestors. As she watched the door opened slowly and a lone figure slipped out. The man, dressed like a sexton all in black and carrying a small lantern, looked around him, drew a large key out of his pocket and locked the door before shuffling off toward the altar.

By this time people were leaving the back of the church and Charlotte could no longer hear rain pattering on the windows. She walked out with the others and made her way home. It was time to cook dinner for Daniel. She had wasted the morning and was no closer to solving the mystery of what happened to Meena than she had been when she started.

As soon as Daniel came home, her feelings burst out. "Oh, Daniel, I'm so worried about what happened to Meena Kaur. The only thing I have learned this morning is that her cook told a delivery man, a coal delivery man, about the important people her master knew. She was just bragging about how important they were but I'm afraid they might have put the family in danger."

"But the old woman who came and picked up Meena was an Indian, wasn't she? She would not have known anything about the coal delivery man."

"That's another strange thing," Charlotte reported. "The cook mentioned that when Meena and Parni got into the carriage, the old woman straightened up and almost lifted them in—'strong as a man' was what she said. Do you think it might have been a man disguised as an old woman?"

"Ah, if it was someone in disguise it could have been anyone—an Englishman or an Indian, any criminal or radical who wanted to get some hold over

Kumar Singh. And I must admit I have found no more information today than you have. Mr. Reynolds, who is such an active Chartist, knows nothing of him. He snorted at the thought of Sikhs coming to London to ask anything of the Queen.

"He talked at length about how British soldiers were slaughtered in the Sikh-Anglo War just a few years ago. A friend of his he said, had been an officer in that army and had never returned after the massacre in 1842. 'If there are any Sikhs in London' he said, 'they had better be watchful lest some British troops want to make them suffer as much as our men suffered' It was an unfortunate conversation."

"Yes, everyone seems filled with anger here in London," Charlotte agreed. "There is almost no subject that can be raised without some people getting angry. Any topic can cause an argument in London. It seems Englishmen don't agree on anything. When we were in America we scarcely heard of these foreign quarrels and wars. It is true, I guess, as our friends in Boston used to say, that it is better to leave the quarrels of the old world behind. America offers a new beginning. But now that we are in London, we are in the midst of it."

When Tom came home, Charlotte questioned him more about what he was doing in the church.

"I never took you for a religious man," said Daniel jokingly. "I thought you would be more likely to take your meal in a pub than in a church. Did your sister set you a good example?"

Betty spoke up, "I have been trying to get him to go to church with me ever since we started courting. When we have children he should set a good example to them."

"But I don't have to start now, because we have no children. I can't say I am eager to go to church and listen to the parsons. Jock says the church oppresses the poor just as the government does. The church collects tithes and we must pay to have preachers tell us to be good even when we don't have enough money for food or clothes."

"Why choose a church then for your rest time?" asked Charlotte. She was becoming quite curious about Tom's new behavior.

"All right, all right. I'll tell you what my mates and I are up too, but you're not to tell anyone else about it. Jock and some of the others are talking about having a great meeting outside of Buckingham Palace, something that will show the Queen what her people really think. She comes and goes in her fancy carriage and never sees how people are suffering. And her foreign husband knows nothing about England. Why should he care? He is just a German prince, they say, and cares nothing about us."

"What will you do at the meeting?"

"We will have speeches by people who know what's going on. People who have suffered because the machines took away our jobs. Thousands of people are wandering the country looking for work on farms and in the cities, but there's no work for them because the machines are doing it all."

"But what has this to do with being in the church?"

"We found a secret place to meet. We need a place where we can store the things we'll need for the meeting—signs and broadsheets to deliver. And Jock knows the sexton at the church. He's a radical too and he lets us meet in the crypt. It's quiet and secret there. Very few people go down there these days."

"You weren't in the crypt today," Charlotte objected. "You were sitting in the pews like everyone else."

"Ah, the crypt was locked when we got there. Jock said we couldn't get in today. No one was at the church to open it up."

Betty was distressed by the talk about demonstrations. "But you will get into trouble. All of you will if you call meetings at Buckingham Palace. Last time you went to a demonstration you were arrested. Oh, Tom, it's terrible danger you'll be in." She threw her arms around him.

"It is dangerous business," Daniel agreed. "You could be charged with treason if your meetings seem to threaten the Queen. This friend of yours, Jock, sounds like a hothead who could get you into real trouble."

"Well, it's time for the common people to control their own destiny. And our leaders are educated men. Maybe they didn't go to fancy schools, but they read and they know things. They will lead us aright. One of them taught us this poem

Men of England, wherefore plough
For the lords who lay ye low?
Wherefore weave with toil and care
The rich robes your tyrants wear?

Charlotte had never seen Tom so excited and so certain about anything before this. But she was worried that his new friends might lead him into far more trouble than he was ready for.

CHAPTER EIGHTEEN

Opening the Church

The next day Charlotte decided she had better go to see whether Meena might have returned during the night. Had Kumar Singh thought to notify the women in her class that it had been cancelled? She couldn't teach the class as though nothing had happened when Meena Kaur was not there.

Rahil opened the door when she knocked. When he saw who it was, he said urgently. "Please come inside. Mr. Singh asked me to tell you about what has happened."

The look of distress on his face told Charlotte that the news was not good. She caught her breath as she waited. Rahil disappeared for a moment and soon returned with a sheet of paper.

"I was making a copy of this note to take to your husband. Mr. Singh said Mr. Gallagher might be able to help in this case." He handed the note to Charlotte.

The paper on which it was written was thin and the bottom had been torn off carelessly. The writing was clear enough, but sprawling, as though it were written

167

by one of her students or someone else unaccustomed
to writing.

If you want your wife returned safely to you, leave
500 pounds in cash in a package marked for "Captain
Saxon" with the barman at the Old Ship pub on the
quayside before dusk tomorrow. Unless you do this,
you will never see her again.

Charlotte gasped when she read the message. "What
has Mr. Singh done? Surely now he wants to inform the
police about what has happened."

"Mr. Singh has gone to speak to a man of some
influence whom he met on the ship coming here from
India. He still does not want to call the police, but he
told me he hoped that diplomats might have some
influence in having his wife's disappearance
investigated."

When Charlotte asked about her class, Rahil assured
her he had sent information to each of the families
where the women worked so they would know that
classes were cancelled. Charlotte wrote a note to
Kumar Singh inviting him to visit that evening to
discuss these latest events. She hoped something would
happen during the day that would provide some good
news.

Then she turned toward St. Barnabas Church. The
story Tom had told her the night before about his
friends meeting in the crypt had started her thinking. If

Tom's radical friends were meeting in the crypt of the church, perhaps other radicals were too. Perhaps the crypt was the key. A crypt was a good place to hide things, Tom said. It would also be a perfect place to hold prisoners. Crypts in most churches have only a few small windows at ground level. The tombs lay undisturbed and might not be visited more than once or twice a year. Perhaps they were scarcely ever visited at all because the area around the church, which had once been filled with large mansions, was now occupied by poor immigrants and rural poor who had no ancestors buried in the church. How could Charlotte find out whether Meena and Parni were being held there?

The square in front of the church was bustling with peddlers and entertainers trying to make a few pennies by singing or dancing on the street. Charlotte wondered whether any of them had seen anything connected with the kidnapping. She noticed a group of women who were gathered around a young man singing a mournful song:

> *Fair Lucy she sits at her father's door,*
> *A-weeping and making moan,*
> *And by there came her brother dear:*
> *'What ails thee, Lucy Wan?'*

No one paid attention to Charlotte. There was no one to question about a possible kidnapping. Too many people were striding busily or wandering aimlessly back and forth across the square for anyone to notice a few extra men or a carriage with two young women. Charlotte walked toward the door into the church, but as she did she saw the same two old women who had been sheltering there the last time she visited. Did they spend all their time there? They might have seen something strange going on. She stopped and smiled at one of them.

"I am wondering whether you might have noticed two young women, strangers in foreign clothes, anywhere about the church in the last few days. Two of my friends are lost and missing in this big city. I don't know where to find them."

One of the women ignored her and sat mumbling to herself and staring down into her lap. The other woman looked up with a sly grin. "Me pipe is out of tobaccy," she said. "Maybe if I was to have a quiet smoke I could remember."

"Here, buy yourself some tobacco," Charlotte responded handing her a coin. "If you can give me any news of my friends, you can have more smokes."

"You remember yesterday, the rain was coming hard?" the woman answered. "It was pouring in the doorway here and I went inside to stay dry. Up by the statue of the bishop I was sitting waiting for the rain to pass and I heard a kind of wail came out of the wall. Weird it was."

"Did it have any words to it, this wail?"

"No, just an odd sound like an animal that was sad and crying to get out. Right by the door of the crypt it was. It must have been a ghost of someone long dead. I'll not let you out of your grave, I thought. We want no ghosts haunting us here. And I hurried back to the door here just as fast as I could."

Charlotte shivered as she heard the story. She gave the woman another coin and hurried toward the crypt. There was no sound now. Charlotte examined the ancient wooden door, now blackened with soot from years of candle smoke. The wood had dried and shrunk from age and Charlotte wondered whether there would be room to slip a piece of paper between the boards. She had no paper with her today, so she knocked on the door quietly enough not to call attention to herself, but firmly. She leaned toward one of the cracks and called, "Are you there? Is anyone there?"

Was that a tiny wailing sound she heard? She couldn't tell. In despair she decided she would have to go outside and try to find some paper for a note. As she turned away, she saw a tiny speck of white between two boards in the door. It moved, and a little more white showed. Someone was pushing a sheet of paper through. Eagerly she went toward the door and helped pull the sheet through. At last she had it. There was the message, sharp and clear:

"HELP Yankee Doodle"

It was a message to her! Meena and Parni were there. Now all she needed was a way to get them out! The door to the crypt was heavy and the lock, although rusty, was massive and looked strong. She tried putting her shoulder to the door and pushing as hard as she could, but nothing budged. Should she wait until Daniel could come and help? Then she thought of the silent sexton she had seen leaving the crypt and locking the door behind him. She must find him and persuade him to open the door for her. She walked toward the front of the church thinking the sexton might be cleaning the area behind the altar, or trimming candles for use in the evening service.

The shadows were deep as she walked behind the altar. By this time the church was nearly empty. The rain had stopped and people went outside to enjoy the good weather. "Is anyone here?" Charlotte called softly as she went. There was no answer, not even an echo from the stone walls. No sound disturbed the gloom.

Disappointed, Charlotte made her way toward the entrance to the church, pondering what she could do next. Then she caught a glimpse of a dark-clad figure coming in through a side door near the altar. Could that be the sexton? She walked back toward him, catching him as he was about to disappear behind the altar.

"Please, are you the sexton?" Charlotte called.

"What do you want with the sexton?" answered a gruff voice.

"I have reason to believe that some friends of mine may have be hidden in the crypt of this church. If they are, I am sure you want to release the two ladies. Would you open the door of the crypt for me?"

The man came a bit closer and peered into her face. "How would two ladies get into the crypt? Where did you ever hear such things as these?" His voice was not only gruff. It sounded angry.

"There was a note," Charlotte wondered why the man was not more eager to help her. Surely any sexton would want to be sure no part of his church was being misused. What was the matter with this man?

"I will have to ask the parson. I've never heard of such goings-on," the sexton finally answered.

"Please just unlock the crypt and let me take a look," she said with as much authority as she could muster. "We cannot waste time. Do you want me to call the police and ask them to break down the door?"

"Don't you think of doing no such thing," growled the sexton. He smiled maliciously at her, "Here, just follow me. I'll show you the crypt."

They walked over to the crypt door and the sexton took the large iron key off his belt and inserted it in the lock. It took strength to twist the key, but finally it turned with a groaning sound and the sexton removed the padlock. He swung open the heavy door and Charlotte could see a flight of stone steps leading downward. She turned to ask for a lantern, but stopped when she saw the hateful expression on the man's face.

"There you are, my lady. Go down and find your friends," he said as he pointed toward the stairs. Charlotte opened her mouth to scream, but only a small cry came out as she felt herself slipping down the first several steps. She heard the door clang shut behind her as she clutched one of the slippery stone steps to keep herself from falling all the way down.

There was no light and no sound. Charlotte ran her hand over the clammy step on which she sat and stared into the darkness. Was anyone there? Perhaps she had made a dreadful mistake. Now she was a prisoner. How would Daniel ever find her?

########

When Daniel returned to his house for dinner that noontime, there were no sounds from the kitchen, no response when he called "Hello, Charlotte!" He walked down the dark stairway to the kitchen but found it cold and empty. The stove had not been lit and there was no sign of food. Suddenly he was worried that Charlotte might have slipped into the sorrowful depths she had been in when they first arrived. He hurried upstairs—no one in the parlor; no one in the bedroom. Where was Charlotte?

It was unlike Charlotte not to have left a note. Could she have disappeared as Meena Kaur had? He went down to the hallway and then noticed a small, hand-delivered note on the floor in front of the door. He opened it and read "If you want your wife…" The ransom demand was for Meena Kaur but fear clutched at his throat as he read it. Had the same thing happened to Charlotte? Had she seen the note before she left? He must walk over to the Singh's house and find out what had happened.

With every step that he took he felt worse. What could have happened to Charlotte? Could she have been kidnapped? But he was not a rich man. Never in this world would he be able to raise 500 pounds to ransom her. And if these strangers held her, what would they do to her? Were they punishing her and tormenting her even now as he tried to keep from running pell-mell to Kumar Singh's house? He had to keep calm. He had to find Charlotte. Perhaps Meena had been rescued and Charlotte was staying with her.

Finally he reached the house and knocked sharply on the door. Rahil answered the door. His smooth brown face gave no indication of emotion. Daniel felt like shaking the man, but he restrained himself and asked merely whether he had seen Mrs. Gallagher.

"Yes, sir," the servant answered. "She was here earlier and asked about my mistress. I showed her the note we received. I was making a copy of it, which I later delivered to your house. I hope that was not wrong. She read the note and looked very concerned. When she heard that Mr. Singh was not here, she left without saying where she might be going."

"Is Mr. Singh at home?"

"No, he has not returned since he left this morning to visit some acquaintances he thought might be able to help him. He said he would not return until he found out more about where his wife was. Do you wish to leave a message for Mr. Singh?"

"No. That is, yes, I will leave a message. May I have a sheet of paper?"

Rahil produced the paper and Daniel quickly scribbled a note. "Please give this to Mr. Singh if he returns without me. Meanwhile I will try to find him. My wife's absence must be connected with the disappearance of Meena Kaur."

Having learned nothing at all about Charlotte's whereabouts, Daniel tried to quiet his mind enough to think about what she would have done. Her face kept coming up before him and he found it hard to think. He longed to tell her how precious she was to him and how he could not possibly go on without her. The poem he had written for her so many years go came back to him and beat a rhythm in his head

Sad the bird that sings alone,
Flies to wilds, unseen to languish,
Pours, unheard, the ceaseless moan,
And wastes on desert air its anguish!

He tried to remember when he had last written a poem for her. They had such busy lives they seldom talked about such things as love now, but the anguish he felt as he thought of possibly losing her was greater than it had ever been. He could feel tears sting his eye and he tried to beat them back.

CHAPTER NINETEEN

In the Dark

After she heard the door close behind her, Charlotte eased herself carefully down the stone steps. She was surrounded by darkness, but very faintly ahead she could see a dim gray daylight coming from two small windows. The slight slope on which the church stood meant that the far side of the crypt was above ground, allowing room for windows. These made it easier for church workers and visitors to move among the memorial tombs of those buried here. Charlotte breathed easier just seeing the faint light.

"Is anyone here?" she called. Then with a sudden inspiration, she started to sing:

Yankee Doodle went to town
A riding on a pony,
Stuck a feather in his cap
And called it macaroni

She heard the sound of a door opening and caught a glimpse of a lighted room beyond. The crypt had a small vestry located on one side of the large stone room. Inside the vestry five chairs were grouped around a table with a lantern on it. The light was not very bright, but Charlotte could make out two sari-clad women who jumped up and cried out.

"Oh, my friend, it is you!" Meena Kaur cried joyfully. "How did you know we would be here? Is your husband here? Can he get us out of this terrible place?"

Charlotte walked slowly over to the door of the vestry. Meena put her hands together in a prayerful gesture and bowed her head. Charlotte did the same, recognizing the traditional Indian greeting. And Parni stood to the side beaming at both of them.

"Was it Parni who slipped the note out through the door?" asked Charlotte. The girl nodded her head shyly. "It was a wonderful note. I knew at once it must have come from you. But how did you get here? Tell me what happened."

Meena told the story of the old woman who had tricked them into getting into the carriage with her. The woman was actually a man, one of the kidnappers in disguise. As soon as Meena and Parni were safely inside the carriage, it drove off quickly. After a short ride, the women were let out of the carriage in the dark and led into the church and down the stone steps. At first they were blindfolded, but after they were securely locked inside, the blindfolds were removed.

"Have you been injured? What did the villains do to you?"

"They have not hurt us. They have been most respectful. They are English, not Indian, and seem to know very little about us. They believe they will get a large ransom because my husband is wealthy, but he is not as rich as they think he is."

"Where are they now? Do they leave you alone like this very often?"

"The first night they brought us here, they threw down some blankets on the floor and told us to sleep there. They stayed awake all night, I think, and watched us, but I was so tired that I slept. After that they took turns going out, but sometimes they both went out. There is no way we can escape. Both Parni and I have climbed those stairs and pounded on the door, but no one ever hears us. And the windows are too high to reach. Someone needs to come and find us. Does my husband know I am here? Will your husband come and rescue us?"

Meena's voice trembled a bit as she spoke. Despite her brave talk, she was clearly very frightened. She seized Charlotte's hand and gripped it tightly. "Tell me that our men are coming. They are brave men. They will break down the walls and rescue us."

Charlotte didn't know what to say. She had not told Daniel where she was going. Why had she been so foolish? Why had she not realized how dangerous it would be? She had assumed the sexton would help her at the church, or even the pastor. But the sexton seemed to be part of the plot and the parson had not appeared at all. How many people were involved in this plot?

"How many men were there in the carriage when you were kidnapped?"

Meena glanced at Parni and then answered. "There was just the man sitting opposite us, and the old woman, who turned out to be a man. And the man who drove the carriage."

"Have these three men been the ones who are holding you captive? Are they the ones who guard you here and bring you food? Have you seen any others?"

"There are only two men we have seen since they brought us here," Meena explained. "When we got out of the carriage, they pulled us roughly into the church and down the steps into this horrid place. We were blindfolded, as I told you. But I do not think there were more than two men who took us out of the carriage.

"They brought us into this little room here and set the lantern down. 'You needn't be afraid of us, ladies,' the man said as he took off our blindfolds, 'As long as your husband is reasonable, we'll treat you just fine.' And they have done that. They have given us a supply of candles as well as the lantern, so we never lack for light and they have brought us food."

"Nasty English food. Not what I like," Parni added.

"We have been well treated, but we are prisoners. Where is my husband? Can he not bring troops to fight these kidnappers and save us? Sikhs are great warriors and that is what we need now." Meena's young voice sounded petulant.

"Your husband does not know where you are. And neither does mine," Charlotte told her soberly. "It was just by accident that I saw the sexton lock the door of this crypt when I was here before. And when my brother told me his radical friends were holding secret meetings in the church, I realized the crypt would be a wonderful secret place to hide someone. But I did not tell anyone else about that."

"How are we ever to get out?" wailed Parni.

"We will find a way," Charlotte reassured her. "Perhaps with three of us, we will be able to open the window and climb out." She looked around the small vestry wondering whether there was a ladder or a key to unlock the window. All she saw was a small table against the wall with shards of broken vases and a few parcels wrapped in dirty cloths.

They took the lantern and left the vestry to walk around the walls of the crypt. The marble plaques marking the burial places of aristocratic Englishmen were all around the walls. Charlotte noticed an urn with wilting flowers in front of one of them. Some people at least must enter the crypt sometimes to leave a token of remembrance. Would that be a way of getting help?

The small windows at the far end of the crypt let in some light from outside but were not designed to open at all. The only way to escape would be to smash the heavy glass and crawl over the shards. They would no doubt bleed to death before escaping.

A clatter on the stairs broke their silence and in a moment two burly men had climbed down. They wore scarves tied around their faces, and their voices were muffled by the cloth. "Are ye thinking of leaving us, ladies?" asked one gruffly. "Put that notion out of your heads. There's a family party coming down now to lay a wreath, but I don't think you'll disturb them. Just come this way."

One of the men took hold of Charlotte's shoulders and pushed her roughly back into the vestry, while the other one seized Meena with one hand and Parni with the other. Both of them were so slight they offered no resistance and soon the three women were inside the vestry. The men took a coil of rope from the corner and methodically tied Charlotte's hands and then the other two. At that moment Charlotte realized they must be sailors or dock workers accustomed to securing crates and boxes on the deck of a ship. Perhaps if we scream loudly, the visitors will hear us, she thought, but a moment later she felt a length of cord tied round her mouth to gag her. As soon as the women were securely tied, the two men left and slipped out of the crypt.

Only a few minutes later, Charlotte heard noises outside and realized that several people were clattering down the stairs. "Light more candles!" she heard someone say. Evidently the workers complied, because they soon heard a man's voice reading Bible verses. *"The souls of the just are in the hand of God and no torment shall touch them."*

Charlotte was afraid the people who were laying the wreath would not stay very long in the dank crypt. She worked desperately to get her hands free from her rope, but the knot was too tight. She spoke through her gag, but the sound came out more like a grunt "Untie, untie…" Then she felt Parni's slight body leaning against her and she realized the child was trying to untie the knot that bound Charlotte's hands. Parni had managed to wriggle her small hands free from the rope that bound them and now she was trying to untie Charlotte's hands.

"If we walk together, we can get out," Charlotte muttered in an urgent whisper through her gag. The rope that circled around them held the three of them tight, but Parni's hands were free and when they reached the door, she could pull it open. Light from a dozen candles looked dazzling to their eyes as they stared into the body of the crypt. Five or six people were standing with their backs toward them, looking at a tombstone set in the wall while one man leaned over a wreath he had placed beneath it.

The three women inched their way toward them, and the tallest man in the group turned toward them. "What is this? Are you ghosts? Or evil spirits?" The two women in the group began to scream, but the tall man peered at Charlotte and then calmly untied her gag and listened to what she had to say.

"Help us, please .We are not ghosts, but prisoners," Charlotte cried. "We are respectable women who have been captured by criminals."

The tall man, who seemed to be taking charge, turned toward the parson. "We have discovered a crime being committed in your church, Reverend. We must free these women and call the authorities."

Several members of the group crowded around to offer help and the rope was soon untied and the gags out of their mouths. As Charlotte rubbed her wrists to get the circulation started again in her hands, she tried to explain what had happened.

"My friend, Meena Kaur, was kidnapped by wicked men who hid her and her servant here while they demanded ransom of her husband. When I came trying to find her, they tricked me into looking down into the crypt and then imprisoned me here too. They left us tied up in the vestry when they heard you coming. But they must have run up into the church. Perhaps we can catch them," she urged.

Most of the visitors just stared at Charlotte as these words tumbled out. She didn't have time to explain more. Instead, she scrambled up the stairs, followed by the tall man and Meena. The church was dark now. Candles were lit here and there around the sides and a little moonlight came through the tall windows, but there were shadowy places everywhere and a dozen men could easily be hidden. Charlotte realized the chase was hopeless.

The tall man had been conferring with the parson. He turned toward the women again. "If you will come with us to the parish house, you can rest a bit and send word to your husbands to come and get you. My name is Robert Carpenter and I am a solicitor and a deacon in this church and this is the Reverend Theodore Smithson, pastor of St. Barnabas. We will certainly investigate and get to the bottom of these mysterious goings on in this sacred building."

A few minutes later, the three women were sitting in the comfortable parlor of the parish house, while the housekeeper brought them tea and biscuits. Mr. Carpenter had sent his coachman to collect Daniel and Kumar Singh and bring them back so they could see that their wives were safe again. Charlotte could scarcely believe that the rescue had happened so quickly, and Meena and Parni looked quite dazed with the sudden change

CHAPTER TWENTY

A Joyful Reunion

When Daniel and Kumar arrived, their faces reflected the joy they felt at seeing their wives safe again. Charlotte could sense Daniel's relief in the heartfelt embrace he gave her and the way he held onto her hand as though he never wanted to let go. Kumar Singh was more restrained when he greeted Meena, not touching her at all, but only smiling broadly and clasping his hands together.   Charlotte had sometimes wondered whether Kumar Singh and his wife were as close as she and Daniel were. Meena had told her that her father had "given her to Kumar Singh as a wife", something that Charlotte would never have accepted. But when she saw the look of affection and joy on Kumar Singh's face, she decided their marriage had grown into something far more than merely an arrangement made by the family.

Telling the story of the kidnapping and then Charlotte's tale of how she had decided to investigate the crypt took some time. "How could you have been so foolish as to try to rescue the women by yourself?"

asked Daniel. And Kumar Singh added, "I admire your courage Mrs. Gallagher. In a different world, you would have made a wonderful Sikh heroine."

After the tale was told, Reverend Smithson wanted to move on to the next issue. "Who are the men who committed this crime? It was not the sexton of the church who opened the crypt for you, Mrs. Gallagher, but an imposter. Our sexton has been ill this past month and has not been attending to his duties. Someone must have been playing a role."

Robert Carpenter spoke up in an authoritative voice, "A serious crime has been committed against a stranger in our midst. The perpetrators must be punished. Can you describe these men to us?"

Neither Charlotte nor Meena Kaur could give them much information. Charlotte remembered the dark clothes of the false sexton, but she had not paid much attention to his face. She was too busy trying to discover where her friends could be. And Meena remembered even less. "They were Englishmen with harsh voices and strong arms," she said. "I could scarcely see them in the carriage and when we were in the crypt, there was very little light."

"I remember their hands," Parni spoke up softly. "Their hands were hard and callused like my father's hands. He was a fisherman and his hands had turned to leather by all the pulling he did on the heavy nets. These men seemed like fishermen or farmers. And one man had lost a finger—this little finger on the end. That can happen when you slice fish open after a heavy catch."

"You have a careful eye, child," said Kumar Singh gently. "Did you notice anything else about the men?"

"They liked newspapers. One man brought in some baked potatoes wrapped in a newspaper and he said, 'We'll be in the *Northern Star* soon. You can read about yourself.' I tried to read what the paper said, but the other man pulled it away from me and crumpled it up."

"The *Northern Star*," said Carpenter. "That's a Chartist paper. Were these men radicals trying to raise money for a radical cause?"

"If they were, they didn't get very far." Daniel was scornful. "I will speak to the editor of my paper the *London Illustrated Weekly*. He is a supporter of the Chartists, but he would never condone criminal activities."

"Ah, but you forget, sir," Mr. Carpenter spoke in his rich, authoritative voice, "these are poor working men—fishermen perhaps as this young girl suggests. Once you inflame the minds of people like that, they inevitably go too far. Have you forgotten the lessons of the French Revolution? You cannot trust the people in the street to remain steadfast for liberty and justice. They will seize the bit in their teeth like untrained horses and will commit not only crimes, but veritable atrocities that can lead to chaos in the cities and throughout the nation. I was unaware that you worked for the *London Illustrated Weekly*, sir, and I cannot say that I admire that newspaper. Mr. Reynolds is a gentleman, but the same cannot be said for all of his followers."

The Reverend Smithson played peacemaker and said, "We need not debate the merits or failures of the Chartists or other reformers. The immediate task is to discover who has committed this outrageous kidnapping. The miscreants should be punished."

"We should perhaps notify the police," suggested Charlotte. All of the men disagreed.

"The police in London can scarcely find the perpetrator of a crime that is committed before their eyes. They have very little power to conduct investigations and question people because the common people are as apt to turn against the police as to help them," Robert Carpenter sounded scornful. "The only thing we can do now is let these ladies return to their homes. The parson and I will question the sexton and people linked to the church to see whether we can get any information about the criminals."

The two couples followed his advice and were soon back in the comfort of their homes. Charlotte and Daniel were welcomed by Tom and Betty who had arrived home from work. Then the whole story had to be told again. Tom was quite indignant at the idea that his friends might have been involved in the kidnapping.

"You said that Jock and his friends met in the church," Daniel pointed out. "They knew the building and might have hit upon the crypt as a good hiding place."

"Possibly", admitted Tom slowly. "Walter as much as said that he had 'borrowed' the key from the parson once to hide something. He said it was just hanging on a hook in the pulpit so that the sexton could find it quickly."

"If they knew the key was there, other people probably knew too," Charlotte mused. "But there is no way of knowing exactly who did know."

"Wouldn't you have recognized their voices if it was Jock and Walter who were there?" asked Daniel. "We certainly heard them talk while they were here, especially Jock."

"There was only one man who spoke directly to me," Charlotte responded. "That was the man dressed as the sexton. He kept his head down and spoke in low, gruff tones. But I was so worried about Meena and Parni that I paid no attention to him. I couldn't even tell you what he looked like. And in the crypt the light was so dim it was difficult to recognize anyone. When the men tied us up, they said a few words, but I scarcely heard them."

Betty spoke up indignantly, "Charlotte, you cannot be saying that Tom's friends might be criminals. Jock and Walter were such cheerful guests when they were here that I can't believe they would do such a terrible thing. Tom, why don't you defend your friends?"

Tom spoke slowly and thoughtfully, "They are both good men, but they do believe very strongly in their radical ideas. I have heard them talk…" his voice slowed and stopped.

"You have heard what?" asked Charlotte sharply.

"I must admit they talked about doing wicked things. They talked about killing the Queen's husband, Prince Albert. They truly believe that only by doing some violence will they ever get the changes they want. They think if the royal family were killed—the way they were in France—working men could make a living again. "

Charlotte and Daniel exchanged worried glances. "We had better talk to them again," said Daniel. "If they have threatened to assassinate Prince Albert, other people have probably heard them talk just as you have. If Mr. Carpenter and Reverend Smithson are going to investigate this crime, they will no doubt hear about those threats."

"But they don't have guns," Tom protested. "They're talking about someday, not today or tomorrow. And they would never think up a crazy scheme like kidnapping women. They don't even know Kumar Singh. What do they have against him?"

That was the end of talk for the evening, but in the morning after the others had left for work, Charlotte decided she would start her own investigation. The first step was to call on Meena to ask how the two Indian women were recovering from their ordeal.

Meena was sitting in the parlor when Charlotte arrived, sipping a cup of tea and looking as though she had no cares. "Oh, come in, my friend," she cried when Rahil showed Charlotte into the room. "I am so glad to see you. Now we are both safe again and we can continue our classes for the Indian women."

"I am glad you want to continue the classes. I was afraid that the shock of the kidnapping might have made you so uncomfortable that you would not want to do that."

"Oh no, I feel much more brave now than I ever was before. I was very afraid of those horrid men, but you rescued me from them and now I am safely home. You are a woman, just like me, but you are brave and strong. I would like to be that way too. I do not always have to hide away in my home as I did when I was a child."

"But we should try to find out who did this terrible thing."

"No, that is not necessary. My husband says there are many enemies who want to destroy Sikhs. They think that we are brutal and cruel. But we are strong and can withstand their attacks. Sikhs have always been warriors, but we are lovers of peace. We only fight when we are attacked."

Charlotte was impressed by this peaceful attitude. It reminded her of her Quaker friend Abigail Prentice back in Boston. Still, Charlotte was determined to find the reason for the kidnapping. It was not enough to have Meena and Parni safe, she wanted to find out who was responsible for their ordeal. She knew Daniel felt the same way. The men behind the plot should be punished. Surely Kumar Singh would want to demand that they pay some price for the fear and suffering they had caused to his innocent wife and her maid.

As she walked slowly back to her house, Charlotte pondered the questions that troubled her. Tom and Jock and some of the other dock workers wanted to start a revolution. They had even talked about killing the royal family. The men who held Meena and Parni captive were working men. They could have been some of the radicals trying to get money to buy guns and carry out some of their plans. But neither Tom nor Jock—probably not their friends either—would have been able to plan a complicated scheme like this kidnapping. Neither of those men would have known that Meena would respond to a message from a Maharani. Neither of them would have thought of pretending to be an Indian woman. And the role was well-played. Whoever pretended to be a messenger from the maharani knew something about India and Indians. This scheme had been carefully planned but where was the person who had all that background knowledge? Until Walter and Jock were found—if indeed they had been involved— there would be no way of tracking a third person. And what if their suspicions were wrong and Tom's friends knew nothing of this? How could she find out who was responsible?

As she approached Cecil Court, Charlotte felt a gentle tug on her skirt. When she looked down, she saw a small girl holding out a bunch of violets, "Ha'penny for some flowers. Pretty violets, just a ha'penny,". As Charlotte took the violets and handed the child a coin, she realized that money was the key to it all. Everything had happened so quickly that no ransom money had been paid, but the mastermind behind the plot might not know that. There were a few hours left before the ransom was due. She and Daniel could find out who had planned the kidnapping by discovering who looked for the ransom. Who was this Captain Saxon?

CHAPTER TWENTY-ONE

A Surprising Discovery

As soon as Charlotte got home she sat down to figure out the best way to find Captain Saxon. They would need the help of a few other people, but if all went well, they should be able to discover the truth. The note delivered to Kumar had demanded that the ransom money be paid before dusk on this very day. The mysterious Captain Saxon would want to get the ransom money, but what if he sent someone else to collect it? She and Daniel would have to be sure they found the man who had planned the kidnapping. They would have to trick Saxon into revealing his involvement in the plot. Then they could confront him with his guilt.

First, Charlotte and Daniel went to the Singh's house and asked Kumar Singh to prepare a package containing several banknotes. The package also included a note from Kumar saying, *"As you see, this envelope contains half of the money you demanded. I need proof that you are holding my wife. When I see her, I will give you the rest of the money. Please do not delay."*

Kumar took the package to the Old Ship pub and left it with the bar keeper there. The grizzled old man at the bar seemed to be expecting the parcel and said he would give it to Captain Saxon as soon as he came in. "He is usually here by the time the sun sets," the bar keeper added.

As soon as the sun began to sink in the afternoon sky, Daniel headed for the Old Ship pub. He would wait as long as it took to see the man who came to pick up the payment. Now that Charlotte and Meena were safely home, the investigation was no longer a matter of life and death, but Daniel was determined to see justice done. He sipped his ale slowly, trying to watch the door without appearing to stare. Time passed very slowly. Then at last he saw a tall man enter and walk directly toward the bar keeper, who smiled slightly and handed him the package. The man slid it into his jacket pocket, and sat down at a nearby table to read Kumar's note. When Daniel saw his face, he recognized him immediately. It was Captain Hugh Granville, the man who had been so angry about Daniel's article. The same man who had spoken scornfully about Indians at the museum reception and had ridiculed their beliefs.

Captain Granville did not linger long in the pub after reading the note. Leaving half his drink untouched, he left the pub and headed in the direction of St. Barnabas Church. Daniel trailed after him, careful to keep as far behind as he dared. He was certain of the man's destination and was not surprised to arrive at the familiar church door. Captain Granville went into the church and Daniel entered quietly behind him.

The church was full of shadows, despite a shaft of light from the sinking sun that came through a stained glass window over the choir loft and the flickering candles on the altar where the pastor had just finished vespers. Daniel saw Charlotte sitting in a pew close to the door and he silently sat down beside her where he could watch as Captain Granville moved quietly around the side of the church.

The few parishioners who had been attending vespers left. Then came the squeak of the door to the crypt and Captain Granville disappeared into the gloom below. By this time Daniel's eyes had adjusted to the dim light and he could see the outlines of Kumar Singh and Robert Carpenter sitting together in a pew on the other side of the church.

A few minutes later, the door of the crypt protested noisily again as it was swung shut and Captain Granville came into the church. He stood for a minute looking at the altar as though he were seeking an answer to a question. Daniel walked toward him.

"Are you looking for the women you kidnapped, sir?" he asked brusquely. "You did not find what you expected, did you?"

As Daniel said that, Charlotte was watching Granville closely. She saw him thrust something behind his back. "He has a revolver, Daniel," she cried, rising up out of the pew and rushing toward the two men.

Daniel seized the man's arm and pulled from his hand a burlap-wrapped parcel tied with rough twine. "This is not a weapon. What is it?"

By this time Kumar Singh and Robert Carpenter had joined them. Carpenter suggested they all adjourn to Reverend Smithson's study where they would have light and time to talk. When Captain Granville saw the four of them, he lost his swagger and walked quietly with them as they left the church and entered the parish house.

Reverend Smithson invited them to take seats in the large, comfortable parlor. He sat down in a chair next to the fireplace and gestured Robert Carpenter to sit next to him. Charlotte and Daniel chose chairs further back from the fire, while Captain Granville and Kumar Singh remained standing as though ready to react quickly to whatever happened.

"There have been some strange activities taking place in St. Barnabas Church," Smithson said. "Before any accusations are made, let us talk about what has been going on and what needs to be done."

Robert Carpenter, accustomed to appearing in courts of law, soon dominated the discussion. He asked Daniel to place Granville's mysterious parcel on the table and unwrap it. As the dingy burlap wrapping fell away, Daniel removed and lay on the table an intricately carved green jewel, smudged now with handling, but gleaming brightly under the lamp.

"That is my Khanda," said Kumar Singh gravely. "You are the man who stole my family's greatest treasure—the gem my father cherished and his father and grandfather before him. Is this how you return our generosity in inviting you into our home?"

"You talk of your family's honor," retorted Captain Granville. "You do not understand that the honor of my family depends upon me. I must preserve the lands my family have cultivated for many generations. This country is being overrun by foreigners who have no respect for our British traditions. We battle with savages who do not even know how to fight like gentlemen."

"The hour is late," Robert Carpenter reminded them. "We have no time for arguments. There are a few facts we must determine. Did you take this jewel from Mr. Singh's family during the banquet they gave for you and your companions when you were in India?"

"Yes," muttered Captain Granville. "I will not deny that. It was merely one of the spoils of war that I deserved for fighting long and hard with her Majesty's Army. Every officer who fights for the Queen receives some of the treasures that have been won. Have you ever seen the riches of the Indians? The jewels their so-called rajahs flash, the luxurious golden chains with which they drape their women, the jewels even on the harnesses of the horses they ride? Those people flaunt their wealth while honest Englishmen become impoverished."

A dark frown on Robert Carpenter's face stopped this flow of words. "Do you truly believe any honorable British officer should repay the hospitality even of foreigners by stealing from them?"

Hugh Granville scowled and stepped back at this question, but he continued stubbornly arguing. "I sorely need to repair the fortunes of my family. The Granvilles have been a noble family for centuries. My mother was a lady-in-waiting to Queen Charlotte and my grandfather fought against the American rebels for King George. We have served our country for many generations, but my unfortunate father squandered his wealth by gambling with dishonest and unworthy men."

The Reverend Smithson looked at Granville sternly. "But the kidnapping of two innocent young women? Surely that cannot be condoned. Mr. Singh's wife and her maidservant were tricked into going to the church where they endured fear and privation."

"I never intended to harm the women," protested Granville. "I only meant to frighten Singh, so he would go back to India and stop making trouble. I was afraid I would not be able to sell the jewel and raise the money I needed as long as he was in London. He might identify the gem and cause trouble."

"You might have been afraid of trouble, but you are now in far more trouble than you have dreamed of,"

Robert Carpenter said solemnly. "When Mr. Singh and I have told your story to the magistrate, you will be charged with kidnapping and you and your family will be disgraced. You talk of retrieving your family's honor, Captain Granville, but I fear you have lost your honor forever."

Kumar Singh had listened quietly as Granville and Carpenter talked, but now he strode to the center of the room. "No! There will be no charge of kidnapping. You have disgraced yourself, Captain Granville, but we will say no more about this."

Dead silence fell over the room. Daniel and Charlotte stared at their Indian friend and wondered at his words. Robert Carpenter's face grew red and he almost sputtered as he spoke. "Say no more? You are not going to let this rascal get away with frightening and perhaps endangering your wife, are you? What kind of man are you who will not punish those who injure your family? I have never heard of such a thing."

"I am the protector of my wife. It is my duty to keep her safe from any man who might harm her in any way. I know that my wife is an innocent and honorable woman, but she was taken from my home and held captive outside of my protection. The honor of my wife must not be questioned by telling others about this outrage. She has been restored to me untouched and uninjured, along with her young maid. I will not have her name mentioned to the courts nor have her ordeal dragged before a curious public."

He paused and looked around the room. "Gentlemen, and Mrs. Gallagher, I trust you will remain silent about this incident and tell no one what happened. As for you, Captain Granville, I know the shame you feel will seal your lips. If not, you may be sure I will avenge my honor and that of my wife."

CHAPTER TWENTY-TWO

Changing Fortunes

After Kumar Singh made his dramatic speech, he turned his back on Captain Granville, bowed to the others, and left. Charlotte was breathless from the sudden turn of events. Never to mention Meena's kidnapping again? To let it go unpunished? That was not the result she had expected. Kumar's decision seemed like a betrayal of her hopes for justice.

Robert Carpenter was the first person to speak. "Captain Granville, we will of course respect Mr. Singh's strong feelings about this crime, but I have more questions to ask you. There were other men who participated in the kidnapping and imprisonment of the women. I want to know who they were."

"I am not required to answer to you, sir," Granville replied. "This is not a court of law. My business is my own and I do not wish to discuss this unfortunate matter further." With that he too left the room.

Reverend Smithson tried to make the best of the situation. "We must thank the Lord that no injury has been done to innocent women. We may regret that a most disreputable man will not be brought to justice, but God works in mysterious way. No doubt the Lord will bring things right in due time and in His own manner."

Charlotte and Daniel made their way home through the dark streets. Neither of them spoke until they were close to Cecil Court. Finally Charlotte said with a sigh, " I suppose we must be satisfied with what we have done. Meena and Parni are safe. Kumar Singh has his family treasure restored. I am sorry Captain Granville will not be punished as he should be, but our hands are tied. If you can't report the kidnapping in the press, what hope is there that we will ever discover who Granville's accomplices were?"

"It all seems wrong," Daniel argued. "There must be something we can do to make it right."

Sunday morning dawned bright and clear. Charlotte woke early and looked with satisfaction on the green buds swelling on the stunted tree that stood in their tiny area in front of the kitchen. The soot and grime of the city made breathing difficult and dimmed the normal sunlight of spring, but even here the flowers would bloom when their time came.

"Let's go for a walk, Daniel," she suggested. "Sunday is the only day of the week when we can go out together. Let's not waste such a fine day. It will cheer us up after yesterday's disappointment."

"We should take a trip into the country soon and get out of this dirty city. Wouldn't you like to see truly green grass and bright flowers instead of these spindly city plants?"

"Someday we will be able to drive into the country in a carriage. When you are a famous journalist, we will be able to travel anywhere we want, but today let's just walk along the river."

Just then Tom and Betty came into the kitchen. The women made tea and Charlotte broiled some bacon while Betty sliced bread for breakfast. Even though Charlotte and Daniel had told them the night before about the kidnapping, Tom could not stop talking about it.

"I was tossing and turning for half the night last night trying to get my mind around this story," he said. "You think that Jock or Walter were mixed up in this business, don't you?" he asked. "I would take an oath that Jock is an honest man. He may be a radical, but he only wants to get rid of the aristocrats. He wouldn't hurt people, especially women. I don't believe he would."

"What about that Walter McGuire who came here with him?" Charlotte asked. "Have you been talking to him recently? You don't know him very well, do you Tom? Maybe he's more dangerous than you think."

"I haven't seen either of them for a while. They haven't been around the docks these last few days. And Walter is usually a quiet one. He listens while Jock goes on and on talking about how the people are going to get their rights at last. He's got strong ideas though, and he knows lots of radical songs. He's not shy about singing those. Have you heard this one?

A hundred years, a thousand years,
We're marching on the road
The going isn't easy
Yet we've got a heavy load,
We've got a heavy load

He comes from up north and says there are real radicals up there. Walter thinks London men are soft. He admires the soldiers and watches them at Buckingham Palace when they troop the colors."

"Maybe he wants to join the army. I wonder whether he has dreams of becoming a soldier himself. The pay's not half bad compared with working on the docks, but the living is not very comfortable. "

"Not Walter! He told me his brother went for a soldier and never came back. They sent him over to India. The heat was something terrible and up in the mountains the snow was even worse. And the savages they were fighting have no more idea of a fair fight than a ten year old does. That's what Walter says."

"War is always terrible," Daniel remarked. "And some soldiers are bound to get killed."

"Yes, but Walter's brother was slashed to death by a band of natives . His mother got a letter from an officer telling her about it. David fought like a brave man, but he was killed in an ambush on a mountain road. That's a terrible way to die."

After about an hour, Charlotte and Daniel went off for their walk. At first they strolled along the bank of the Thames watching the ships. The shoreline was muddy and dirty with all sorts of floating debris. Charlotte saw dead animals, chunks of rotting wood from derelict buildings, tree branches and even pieces of clothing. Scavengers on shore, holding long poles, were trying to pull in the clothes and anything else they thought they could sell.

"Let's go over to Buckingham Palace and watch the troops," Charlotte suggested. "I've been thinking about why the men who worked with Captain Granville asked for so much money. They must have known that kidnapping was terribly dangerous. Why did they need the money so urgently?"

"Everyone wants money," Daniel remarked. "Captain Granville wanted to pay his father's debts and save his family's estate. He must have spent a lot of time planning the kidnapping. First there was spying to find out how to entice Meena out of the house. He must have asked the cook a lot of questions about how the household worked, so when he disguised himself as an old woman he could persuade the women to leave."

Charlotte agreed. "He had to find a safe place to keep the women. And he had to persuade at least two men to work with him. They bought candles and blankets and food to keep Meena and Parni comfortable. What hold did Captain Granville have over the men who worked with him? Were they only after money? There must be less dangerous ways to get money."

"Yes, only people who are desperate to get a lot of money would do something as dangerous as kidnapping women. Of course, Walter could have agreed, in part, because the Singhs are Indian. It sounds as though his brother's death made him hate the Indians. He might have been glad to get back at an Indian family in revenge for his brother's death. Will we ever be able to get the whole story? Kumar Singh and his beliefs about honor have made it impossible to find out why this happened."

By this time they were close to Buckingham Palace where they could see the military guards marching in formation across the courtyard. Small groups of people were gathered around watching the soldiers in their bright red coats carrying rifles on their shoulders and stepping with precision. High up on a balcony tiny figures watched the troops.

"There is the Queen and Prince Albert," Charlotte pointed them out. "I wonder whether they take the baby princess out to watch the soldiers."

"I don't think babies care very much for soldiers, but there are certainly enough people here who do. Why do you suppose they are so fascinated by marching men?"

They strolled around the open square and Daniel spotted someone who looked familiar. "Is that Walter McGuire over there? He certainly seems to be interested in soldiers. He's staring at them hard enough. Let's see if we can ask him a few questions."

When they got closer, McGuire looked up and saw them. As they moved toward him, he quickly turned away and disappeared into the crowd.

"Well, he is acting like a guilty man all right," Daniel muttered. "But let's not worry about that today. I want to celebrate having you back safely. And I have some news to make you happy. Mr. Reynolds likes my work. He told me he would pay me a bonus for the article I have written about the Chartists. The newspaper is selling better than ever."

"That's wonderful news. I'm so proud of you, Daniel!"

"Ah, but that's not the best part. Now that I have some money, I think it is time we found ourselves a kitchen maid to help you in the house. You shouldn't have to roughen your hands by scrubbing. You should sit in the parlor like a lady."

"I wouldn't be happy if I had no work to do. I am not made to be an idle lady, Daniel Gallagher. You should know that."

"I know you are a wise woman and a wonderful teacher and you should spend your time using your talents, not scrubbing kitchens. You enjoy teaching your classes and perhaps you will be able to write some essays for our newspaper or other journals. I want the whole world to know what an extraordinary wife I have found. When I thought for a little while that I had lost you, the whole world turned black to me. Now that you are safe again, I want to treat you like the treasure you are."

"Oh, Daniel, aren't we lucky? I don't envy the Queen up there on her balcony. She may have a crown, but she cannot be as happy as I am."

Later that afternoon, Charlotte told Betty about the idea of having a servant girl to help with the housework.

"Ooh, you're the lucky one, Charlotte! You found yourself a good husband all right." She tossed her head before continuing, "But I'm sure Tom will get me a kitchen maid when he's had time to save up a bit of money. And I know just the girl who would love to work in your kitchen.

"I met Kathleen O'Reilly the other day. You must remember Deirdre's sister. She came by the laundry when I was working. Looking for a job she was. She went up north to her cousins after Deirdre died in that terrible fire, but she couldn't stay long. Work was hard to find, and the family was so crowded together they didn't want to keep her. Didn't want to give her food. Her cousin as much as told her she should go out on the street and earn the money any way she could to bring something into the house."

"So she's come back to London to get work?"

"Yes, and work is hard to find here too. She's only fifteen and she can scarcely read or write. All she can do is plain housework. And she has no references. She said she might have to go on the street here too—she's pretty enough for a man to want her."

"That's outrageous! We mustn't let that happen. Kathleen is a very bright girl and hard working too. You remember how she started learning to read when she came to my class. Will you be able to find her? Tell her she can come and work for me. I'll teach her to read and write so she'll be able to become a cook if she wants."

The next day Betty brought home a slip of paper with an address scrawled on it. "When Kathleen came to the laundry last week, she told the woman in charge where she could be found if there was work. Here is the address the woman gave me. She said it is a mean neighborhood and I shouldn't go there. Maybe we should send Tom."

Charlotte thought she could manage to find the address given to her, but she wasn't sure Kathleen would still be there. How was she paying for a room? There were very few choices for a girl like Kathleen. It was important to find her quickly wherever she might be.

Early on Wednesday morning Charlotte set off to find Rosemary Lane. When she got there she saw it was a narrow, muddy street with tall houses looming over it. As she walked down one side, she could see that a dozen little lanes and courts led off from the street, making a maze of the numbers on the houses.

They didn't follow each other in any order but wove in and out of courtyards filled with lines of laundry.

In the streets and courtyards, small barefoot children were splashing in the puddles and playing with bits of broken brick and stones. The boys threw pieces at each other and at the girls who huddled in doorways and threw them back. A few of them chanted taunts and sang snatches of songs while they played:

Paddy was a Welshman
Paddy was a thief
Paddy came to my house
And stole a side of beef.
I went to Paddy's house
Paddy wasn't home.
I picked up a fire stick and
Burned his house down.

Charlotte thought about the children she had taught in America and how much they loved singing those old songs and teasing one another. These children were thinner and dirtier than the ones she had in class, but their spirits were high.

After a long search, Charlotte finally found the number she was looking for and knocked on the door of a ground-floor flat. A tired-looking woman with graying hair, who seemed to have only two teeth left in her mouth, opened the door.

"What is it you're wanting, Miss?" she asked.

"I am looking for Kathleen O'Reilly. I was told she lives here." Charlotte could see beyond the woman into the dark room with no furniture except a battered table and two chairs, one of which had only three legs. On the floor was a muddle of shawls and blankets from which a half-asleep man peered at the open door.

"Sure, she went out this morning to find work. If she don't bring back a few coins I can't keep her. There's others would like a place in my lodgings."

"Have you any idea where she is looking?"

"No, I just told her to get out and find something. I can't give charity."

Discouraged Charlotte turned around and left. As she walked past a group of girls leaning against the doorway of the flat next door, she stopped and asked them. "Do you know Kathleen O'Reilly? Do you know where she might be?"

"If I can have a ha'penny, I'll show you," said the oldest girl. Charlotte gave her a coin and the girl led her through the maze of Rosemary Lane out into a large square where a number of food carts stood.

"There she be," said the girl, pointing to the coffee barrow. And Charlotte could see Kathleen standing beside the barrow woman pouring steaming coffee into large cups.

CHAPTER TWENTY-THREE

Planning Changes

When Kathleen O'Reilly saw Charlotte, she smiled. And when she heard that the Gallaghers wanted her to work for them, her face lit up. "Oh, I thought I'd never be able to put up with the crowd in Rosemary Lane. It's not much I ask for, but a clean, quiet place would be so nice. Nothing at all good has happened to me since Deirdre died—rest her soul—and I sometimes thought I'd just lie down on a street and die."

That evening she came to the Gallagher's house, carrying her few belongings wrapped in a plaid shawl. She had another plaid shawl over her shoulders to keep the sharp wind away. Charlotte showed her the tiny room set off the kitchen that would be her bedroom. It was so small there was no room in it for more than a narrow bed and a tiny table. Kathleen beamed when she looked at the dark, chilly room and said cheerfully, "What a wonder it is to have a place of my own. Blessings on you and your husband! My mother will be so glad to hear about this."

The next morning Charlotte walked to the market with Kathleen to help her learn her way around the neighborhood. Kathleen talked about how difficult her life had been since they had left Ireland. "We were poor in Ireland too, and the family was large. After Deirdre and me, my mother had five more children to care for. When we were small we always had enough to eat. My father back then worked hard on the boats. He was a fisherman and the cod were usually plentiful. But he had bad luck.

"One year a storm smashed his boat against the rocks and tore a big hole in the side of it. By the time he managed to get back to harbor, the hole was bigger. Wood is expensive and he couldn't buy enough to mend it, so he had to start going out on other men's boats. It's a pity he had no sons, but God kept sending him daughters. He got discouraged and his work wasn't always good. Some of the men stopped hiring him on to help because he'd be drinking and not always fit to work in the morning. Deirdre and I couldn't find work, so finally my Ma had to take the little ones and go to the workhouse. That's when Deirdre and I came here. Deirdre always took care of me, but now I'm on my own and I feel so alone."

"You're not alone anymore," Charlotte reassured her. "If you work hard and get some education, you'll be able to find a place in one of the big houses here in the city. And you might become a cook and rule over a whole kitchen."

Within a few days Charlotte and Meena Kaur had set up the classes again in the Singh house. Kathleen joined the class and Charlotte noticed her surprise as she stared around the table at the other women who were wearing colorful saris and golden earrings.

"I never thought I would be sitting next to a brown person in a big house like Mrs. Singh's house," she confided to Charlotte and Betty as they walked back home. "And their names sound so strange—Daheela and Indri—and Lord knows what else. I have to twist my tongue around to say them. But for all that, they are girls a lot like me. And to think we are all going to learn to read together!"

The Singhs avoided talking about the kidnapping and the danger Meena had been in. Now that it was over, Kumar Singh did not want to expose his wife to any questioning by English authorities. Charlotte could not quite understand his attitude, but she respected his wishes. Only Daniel chafed at being denied a chance to get to the bottom of a tormenting mystery.

Tom was still finding work at the quays, but Jock and Walter had not appeared there after the kidnapping. Daniel asked about them every evening and became increasingly irritated when Tom continued to have no news.

"Perhaps Jock and Walter are looking for work somewhere else," Charlotte suggested. "The docks along the river stretch for quite a distance. I could go down there and look for them"

"You can't wander along the riverside by yourself," objected Daniel. "People would think you were not a respectable married woman. And I won't have people thinking badly about my wife!"

"But Daniel, I can take Kathleen with me. We'll bring some cakes and sell them to the workers. No one bothers the cake women. The men care more about choosing the cakes."

Daniel was reluctant, but Charlotte persuaded him to let her try. The morning she and Kathleen chose to go, they were up and out of the house before dawn, stopping at the market to buy buns from a sleepy bakery man before setting off toward the river. As they approached the water, the wind picked up a little, but they were so excited they scarcely noticed the chill. It was easy to find workers gathering on the docks waiting to be chosen for a job. Charlotte peered carefully at every face, but saw none that looked familiar. She wondered whether she would recognize Jock unless he was wearing the same clothes he had worn when he visited their house. After walking past dozens of men and selling most of their buns, Charlotte felt more confused than ever. She looked around the crowd of shabby men in despair.

Finally their last bun was sold. Most of the workers who were needed that day had been chosen and others were scattering to look for work elsewhere or go home. Charlotte turned to Kathleen to suggest they should leave too when she heard a familiar voice singing a Chartist ballad:

The time shall come when wrong shall end,
When peasant to peer no more shall bend;

Quickly turning toward the sound, Charlotte saw Jock and Walter wandering slowly across the dock. Before they saw her, she was beside them, greeting them with a smile.

"Why Jock Fisher and Walter McGuire, we've been looking for you two. I'm Mrs. Gallagher. Do you remember me? And this is Kathleen O'Reilly. My brother Tom is eager to see you again. He has been talking about you and some of your ideas, but he said he hasn't seen you working on the docks for a while."

"We had some other work to do," mumbled Jock, looking suspiciously at Charlotte. But when she said nothing, he added, "We'd be happy enough to see Tom again. Maybe we should go back to work on that stretch of docks one of these days."

"Oh, do that!" Charlotte encouraged them. "And my husband and I would like to have you come for another visit soon."

Within a couple of days Jock and Walter started working again on the docks with Tom again, although they did not take up Charlotte's invitation to visit. Tom saw them often and, at Daniel's urging, asked them a few questions about what they had been doing during their abrupt disappearance from the docks.

"There is more revolutionary activity going on in this city than you know about," Jock told Tom mysteriously. "It's best not to get involved in too many schemes. Sometimes they don't work out as well as they should."

"But no harm's done," Walter added. "And we'll keep working for the revolution. We have a couple of things up our sleeves." But he refused to say anything more about their plans.

Tom was becoming more and more radical in his ideas. His friends at work had not only given him new ideas about how the world should run, they had also filled him with more ambition than he had ever had in his earlier rural life. Every night he and Betty would pore over the reading materials Charlotte gave them and practice reading and writing.

Charlotte was pleased that Tom was working and studying now, but she worried that his friends might get him into trouble. She was pretty sure Jock and Walter had been part of the kidnapping plot, but there was no proof and she and Daniel had promised to say nothing about it.

"I'm almost certain the two of them were mixed up with Captain Granville," she complained to Daniel one evening. "I hate thinking that they could do such a thing. And now they are Tom's best friends. I hoped they might say something to him about the kidnapping, but they've never said a word about it or explained why they were away for several days."

"We have no way of proving they were involved," Daniel pointed out. "And if we could prove it, what could we do? The police don't even know about the kidnapping. No one will ever be punished for that crime, I'm afraid."

"Too many bad things had happened since we came to London, Daniel. Yesterday when I was peeling potatoes with Kathleen, she started crying. She misses Deirdre so much and thinks about her all the time. No one has ever been punished for Deirdre's death either, but I'm sure it was not just an accident."

"No, we'll probably never know what happened to Deirdre," Daniel admitted. "Your search for that mysterious peddler never led to anything, did it?"

"No, I found nothing. Terrible things have happened and there's been nothing we could do about it. We don't believe Deirdre's death was an accident, but how can we learn the truth? So many questions we can't answer. It makes me feel useless."

"Useless? That's the last thing you should think about yourself. You've done so much, Charlotte! You rescued Meena and Parni when no one else could find them. And you've been teaching people to read. That's good too. Those women in your class will bless you forever."

"It's not enough, Daniel. I feel like a failure. Everything has gone wrong since we lost Brian. And then my mother. It seems as though every day has been worse since then."

"We've had a difficult time since we got to London, haven't we? But we'll get through it together. You need a change, Charlotte. Now that the weather is getting a little warmer perhaps it's time we took a trip to Bristol. You said you wanted to visit your mother's grave and I'm going to take you there."

"How can you take time off to go to Bristol?"

"We'll go by train. You forget how fast those are now. The railroad is advertising their schedules in my newspaper. We could leave on the early morning train next Sunday and get down there, visit the grave, and take a late train back."

CHAPTER TWENTY-FOUR

A Visit to the Country

Sunday's skies promised good weather, although it was still dark when Charlotte and Daniel left Cecil Court and walked to the railroad station. They chose the cheapest tickets and Charlotte was grateful to Parliament for having passed a law requiring all railroads to offer third class travel. Soon perhaps even Betty and Tom would be able to ride on trains and speed through the countryside. But four hours of jostling on a hard wooden seat, eating the dry bread and cheese Charlotte had packed for them, was enough. When the train drew into the Bristol station, she was glad to get off and walk on solid ground again, clutching the battered flowers she had brought to put on her mother's grave.

As she and Daniel walked toward the exit to hand in their tickets, she saw a familiar figure descending from a first class carriage.

"Isn't that Captain Granville?" she asked Daniel excitedly.

"It certainly is. I'm glad we won't have to face him again. Look, someone has sent a carriage to take him off to wherever he is going."

The streets were Sunday quiet as Charlotte and Daniel walked away from the central city and toward the outskirts. Much had changed since Charlotte had last seen the city twelve years earlier, but as they left the paved streets and started walking on the dirt roads between hedgerows, the scene was more familiar.

"There's the church we used to go to. I don't suppose Reverend Carter is still there, but my father is buried in that churchyard and my mother will be too, I'm sure."

They could hear the congregation singing a closing hymn; the service was just ending as they walked through the small churchyard and found the inconspicuous stone marked "Sacred to the memory of Thomas Edgerton" and beneath it, in smaller letters the more recent addition "and his beloved wife, Mary". After laying the flowers on the ground in front of the stone, Charlotte and Daniel stood silently for a few minutes until they heard the sound of voices as the service ended and parishioners emerged from the church.

Charlotte watched as people streamed out the doors, stopping to speak briefly to the minister, who looked much younger than any minister Charlotte remembered seeing as a child. None of the dark-clad women in their best dresses nor their husbands in Sunday jackets looked familiar to her. But then she noticed a young woman's face and smiled as she recognized her.

"Oh, Daniel. There is my friend Molly. I've known her all my life. I must speak to her." Charlotte approached a slender woman in a dark green dress. When the woman looked up and saw Charlotte, she smiled broadly.

"Is that you, Charlotte Edgerton? I scarcely recognized you looking so blooming. It's been many a year since I've seen you."

"Twelve years it is, Molly, since I left. And I'm not Charlotte Edgerton any more. This is my husband, Daniel Gallagher."

The three of them walked slowly across the churchyard exchanging news. "You were lucky to get away from here, Charlotte. You look healthy and happy. Things didn't go so well for me. I married Jeb Cooper from over Newport way, but during the hard winter we had in '38, he caught a fever and died. And I've been scrambling on my own ever since. My father and mother are both dead and my brother went off to be a soldier and never came back. I'm lucky I have a place on the big Granville house as a kitchen maid."

"I don't remember the Granville family living around here while I was growing up."

"Oh, this is just one of their places. They have a large house in London and I think the old Lord Granville lived there most of his life. He was a great gambler and his wife liked society, they say. They closed up this house for years, but now that they are gone, the young Lord has moved back here. They've shut up the London house to save money."

"How do you like working there?"

"It's not a bad place. Lord Granville leads a quiet life. His wife died two years ago of consumption and he is not a well man himself. The cook has to make all sorts of fancy dishes for him and he hardly eats them. The cook lets me finish them up in the kitchen. She is good to me most of the time, although she works me very hard. Why don't you come over for a while and sit in the kitchen? It's chilly out here. We'll freeze to death catching up on the news."

The walk to the Granville house was not long and both Charlotte and Daniel enjoyed the brisk air as they strolled along the dirt road bordering fields where early spring crops were beginning to send shoots up into the sun. The songs of birds in the hedgerows and cows mooing in the pasture were sounds they had missed in London. Soon the gray walls of the imposing Granville Hall loomed before them.

Molly took them to the back entrance, where they found a quiet, warm kitchen. Most of the staff were still at church or visiting family. The fire was banked in the large stone fireplace where a large kettle of soup simmered slowly.

"Sit down and tell me about London. Do you really live there? You came back from America? What a lot of places you have seen," Molly leaned forward eagerly.

Charlotte told her about the flat in London where they lived. "And my brother Tom and his wife Betty are staying with us now," she explained. "Tom works on the docks these days and Daniel writes stories for his newspaper about all the things that are going on in the city."

Molly stared Daniel, "You write in a newspaper? Oh, you must know a lot. Just like Lord Granville himself. We use newspapers for kindling sometimes, but I can't make head nor tails out of those black squiggles. Sometimes cook tells me about the stories. Do you ever meet the famous people they write about in the papers?"

"I don't meet many famous people," said Daniel. "I did meet Feargus O'Connor." Molly's face remained blank.

"We've met Lord Granville's brother, Captain Granville," Charlotte added. "That's why I was so surprised to learn that he lives here."

"You met the Captain? Isn't he a handsome man? He spoke to me a few times. Gave me a whole packet of papers that I must burn for him, and he gave me a tuppence. He seems a very generous man."

"Did you burn all the papers?" Charlotte asked. "I wonder why he had so many."

"Letters they were. That's what he said. But they're not burned yet, not most of them anyway. There's a packet of them in the pantry. I'll burn them bit by bit when I need to feed the fire. It's handy to have extra paper."

Charlotte and Daniel looked at each other wordlessly. Did the letters hold some of Captain Granville's secrets about the kidnapping plot? Charlotte made up her mind.

"Captain Granville did a very cruel thing to a friend of ours, Molly. He is not a very nice man and we would like to know whether he has plans to hurt anyone else. Could you show us those letters, Molly?"

"They are nothing but a bunch of old papers. I suppose there's no harm in you seeing them."

The three of them moved into the pantry, a small, dark room with hams hanging from the ceiling and battered milk cans standing on shelves near the door. Molly pulled a small packet of papers from one corner of the shelf and handed them to Daniel. After flicking through the pages for a few minutes, he turned to Charlotte."

"These are letters to his brother, Lord Granville, talking about money. But he mentions Kumar Singh. I wish we had time to read all of them."

"Molly," asked Charlotte impulsively. "Would you give us these papers? They might be important. We can give you some money to buy newspapers to use for your kindling."

"I'm not sure that's right," Molly twisted her hands together in her lap. "What if Captain Granville finds out?"

"They're of no use to him. That's why he gave them to you to burn. I'm sure he doesn't care about them anymore. But they might be of help to a friend of ours. And we could give you a shilling or two to pay for your trouble."

Molly's eyes sparkled as she thought of the money, and the exchange was quickly made. Reluctantly Charlotte and Daniel told Molly they would have to leave to catch the train back to London. Clouds were already blowing in over Bristol and the sun would soon be setting. Charlotte promised to come back for another visit later in the year and she and Daniel walked to the railroad station marveling over their luck in finding more information about Granville.

There was no privacy on the train to read the packet of letters, so Daniel kept them tucked in his jacket pocket. It wasn't until they were safely home that he felt comfortable untying the string wrapped round the pages and spreading them out on the table under the light of their brightest lamp. They looked through the letters, but could not read much. The handwriting was hurried and hard to read in the flickering light.

"I'll try to read them all tomorrow, Daniel, while you are at work. I am sure I'll be able to decipher the handwriting when I have them in the daylight."

Charlotte kept the packet of letters close by her bed overnight and the next morning, as soon as the others had left for work, she turned to them. She carried the sheets to the parlor window and read them by the gray light of the London morning.

My dear Alfred,

I write to tell you that I have settled in a lodging in London. When I returned from India, I expected to find the Granville townhouse available for my use, but I soon discovered that you have leased it to a mill owner from Lancashire. Thank heavens our dear mother did not live to see this day when her lovely carpets would be soiled by Manchester boots.

Do not think I have forgotten the troubles of our family. In fact I have a scheme that will help save us from the embarrassment of facing some of those vile men who hold notes from our father. My service in India gave me some opportunity to acquit myself honorably and gain a few well-deserved rewards. It is not always easy, however, to obtain possession of my bounty. Here in London I have come across an upstart of a kaffir who, I fear, means to deprive me of what is rightfully mine. Fortunately these heathen are not as clever as Anglo-Saxon men and I have hoodwinked him with promises that will never need to be fulfilled.

Now I must be off to meet some fellow-officers. I will write again soon for you may be sure I am not neglecting my family duties.

Your devoted brother,
Hugh Granville

**

My dear Alfred,

Once again I take up my pen to allay your fears that nothing is being done about the troubles that have fallen upon our house. Such is not the case, although I must admit, the time involved is growing longer. The prideful kaffir who I mentioned in my last letter has proved to be impervious to suggestions that he might be placing himself in danger by coming to London and seeking an audience with the Queen. Can you believe the conceit of the fellow to think that Her Majesty would consent to an interview? Perhaps he will suggest that he bring his dusky wife, who is probably barefoot and bejeweled, with him on his visit.

Turning some of the infidels' shabby tricks against them, I decided a good scare might hasten him on his way back to India. Fire is always useful for frightening the ignorant and savage races, so I cleverly arranged for a fire to break out in his kitchen, knowing that it could easily spread throughout the house and cause damage as well as fear. You may have heard of the new ether gas that some of our fellows are using at parties. It makes for a memorable experience but must be handled carefully. And so I handled it. A fire was started that could not possibly be traced back to me. No one saw me except an ignorant young serving girl. Unfortunately, the damage seems to have been less than I had planned. The fire did not spread far enough. I believe the young maid was injured, but the rest of the household remained safe and my heathen friend shows no sign of leaving London.

But I have not given up. I have many plans and you will have reason to thank your brother for his work...

Charlotte turned quickly to the next letter.

Aha, my dear brother. I have made another step forward in my quest to restore not only our family fortunes, but the honor of the British aristocracy. London, as I told you during my last visit, is seething with rebels who wish to gain the vote and change the country. You have no doubt heard of the dubious activities of these Chartists with their arrogant claims that they can run the country rather than letting their betters handle the complex business of governing. But I caught two of these scoundrels in a theft of some guns I was shipping back from India. If I tell the authorities, I can have them both locked up, but I have a better idea.

I am going to use these stout fellows to carry out a scheme I have devised to finally get rid of the kaffir who has caused me so much trouble. I will not set this plan on paper, but you may be sure that you and I will chuckle over it when it has succeeded. And the cleverest part of all is that once I have obtained my rightful booty from India and sent the benighted native back to his wretched homeland, the guilt for the crime will fall on the two radicals who will carry it out. The Queen's justice will fall on them and get them out of my way.

Charlotte gasped with surprise and relief. Here it was—proof that Hugh Granville was responsible, not only for the kidnapping of Meena and Parni, but also the death of Deirdre. She could scarcely wait to tell Daniel the full story and talk about what they could do.

CHAPTER TWENTY-FIVE

Protesting Injustice

When Daniel came home from work, Charlotte and he went over the letters again. "You see, Captain Granville talks almost openly about starting the fire that caused poor Deirdre's death," Charlotte pointed out." And the last letter is surely about the kidnapping. Can we not find some way of prosecuting him for his plans?"

"We promised Kumar Singh never to mention the kidnapping and we must honor that. But perhaps we can persuade the authorities to prosecute Captain Granville for the death of Deirdre. That would be some justice for the poor girl."

"How could we make them change their minds and reopen the case?"

"I am not sure," Daniel admitted. "I think I will speak to Mr. Reynolds. He knows many lawyers and judges. Those influential people might not speak to you or me, but they would listen to him."

Charlotte waited impatiently almost all of the next day to hear what Daniel had to say about his talk with

Mr. Reynolds, but he had no answers. "I spoke to Mr. Reynolds about reopening the inquiry into Deirdre's death. For a few minutes I thought I had persuaded him, but then he shook his head."

"The girl is dead. There has been no outcry. Now you say you have proof that this officer in the Queen's Army is responsible. Does anyone care? Do you suppose a judge will want to create a scandal in order to avenge a young Irish woman? We must choose our fights carefully and not waste time and effort. Ether indeed! So a fire starts—a scullery maid dies. Is it the fault of the fire or of carelessness? Who are we to judge? Can you go to a jury with a case like that?"

When Daniel told Charlotte of Mr. Reynolds's reaction, she sighed with exasperation. "Does he think no one is important enough for justice except people with money and power? We must change his mind."

Days went by, however, and neither Charlotte nor Daniel could think of a way to use Captain Granville's incriminating letters. Daniel suggested he might write an article on the unfair court system, but it would take a long time to find enough cases to present a strong argument.

One evening Tom came home with a scrap of newspaper one of the men had given him. "Look at this! See how honest working people are being tormented by the rich landlords." He shook the paper under Charlotte's face as she sat at the kitchen table.

Ballinglass Incident she read. *300 tenants have been evicted from their homes even denied a chance to pay their rent. Wicked land owner drove them out and tore down their houses simply to make pasture land for her cattle. Will the English government condone such injustice in Ireland? Who is responsible for this outrage? Why does the Queen not protect the subjects she has sworn to defend?*

"Has this really happened?"

"Indeed it has. Many of the newspapers have reported it. And I'm hearing that there will be a great protest soon at Buckingham Palace. Where is the justice in this country?" Tom's face was red with fury.

They were still talking when Daniel came home and confirmed the bad news. "One of Mr. Reynolds's Irish correspondents sent an article to the newspaper about this. And soon afterward, Feargus O'Connor came to our office to submit a letter he wants to have printed. He says the people should rise up about this outrage and demand that the order be rescinded."

"Aye, so they should, but the government is always on the side of the landlords," Tom said. "We should march on the Palace now and demand our rights. When a tenant pays his rent and tends his land, the owner has no right to throw him out without warning. What will happen to those people now?"

"We are going to petition the Prime Minister and demand an investigation into this incident," Daniel told them. "I am to write the petition myself and Mr.

Reynolds will print it. I have much work to do before next week."

For the next week Daniel was busy writing the petition for his newspaper as well as a pamphlet about Ballinglass that could be distributed to people who did not purchase the *London Weekly Newspaper*. During the day he worked at the newspaper office, but in the evening he sat at the kitchen table with Charlotte and wrote his pamphlet.

"Maybe some of your Irish friends who work on the docks can give us background on the conditions in Ireland and tell the story of what happened to the village" Charlotte suggested to Tom.

"They can do that easily enough, but writing a pamphlet is not going to satisfy the Irish workers or Walter McGuire either. He still plans to march on the Palace."

One evening Tom brought another friend over to give Daniel more information. This was a dock worker, Owen Reilly, who had recently arrived from Ireland.

"We were treated like animals," he said. "The English closed our schools and the children could learn nothing unless they went to the English clergy who were teaching them lies. And on top of that, didn't we have to pay tithes to keep those same clergy living in luxury? For every basket of fish my father sold, some of the price had to go to pay the very people who were telling us we were ignorant fools. They stood up in their pulpits and said that the Pope himself was the devil and that the church was the Whore of Babylon. They wouldn't even let us speak our language. It had to be English everywhere."

"My grandmother used to speak the Irish," Kathleen added. "She never would twist her tongue around English. The *sassenach*, that's what she called them."

"I know something about how the English army treated the Irish," added Daniel. "Didn't my own father fight with Wolfe Tone back in '98? Remember the song I sang to you, Charlotte?

Some died by the glenside, some died near a stranger
And wise men have told us their cause was a failure
But they fought for old Ireland and never feared danger
Glory O, Glory O, to the bold Fenian men

That struggle ended badly when my father fought. Now with the potato crop failing all over the countryside, the English will let the Irish die of hunger and never lift a finger to help them."

"But surely you cannot cover all the history of Ireland in your article, can you? You must write about the Ballinglass affair. That is what people are fighting about now," Charlotte reminded him.

Finally the pamphlet was finished and Daniel took it straight to the printer. Tom and his friends promised they would urge all their friends to read it before the big protest demonstration started on Sunday.

"And I'll take it down to Rosemary Lane where so many of the Irish immigrants live," Kathleen promised. "They will want to join in the demonstration."

The following Sunday the dawn was dark and soggy. A surly gray sky hung over London and rain dribbled down, starting and stopping as though even the weather couldn't decide what the day would bring. Charlotte stared out of the small kitchen window into the sodden area way wondering whether people were reading Daniel's pamphlet this morning or thinking about the petition.

A loud rap on the door startled her. She opened it and saw Walter McGuire and Jock Fisher standing outside. "Tell your brother we are going to march to the Palace come what may. The Queen is in residence and we will make our voices heard." After leaving their message, they walked briskly away to rouse other people and encourage them to join the demonstration.

Betty and Kathleen walked over to the market to buy fish for dinner and Tom left to join his mates at the demonstration. Charlotte fussed around the kitchen trying to plan what she would ask Kathleen to cook for dinner, but her thoughts were on what was happening outside. Daniel had left early to meet with Mr. Reynolds and assess any response that was coming in. His article had been an urgent plea for the English government to rescind the order of eviction in Ballinglass As Daniel wrote, *"No civilized country can allow property owners to dispossess tenants who have faithfully paid their rent every year. And no property owner should arbitrarily deny these tenants the right to be sheltered by their neighbors. The Bible has taught each of us that we must love our neighbor as ourselves. Will the government of England ally itself with those who are enemies of common moral beliefs and religious teachings?"*

The article was splendid, Charlotte thought, but she wondered whether the Queen in her palace had thought at all about her dispossessed subjects in faraway Ireland. Feargus O'Connor, Mr. Reynolds, and Daniel were meeting to discuss whether they would join the protest or whether it was better to let the radical workers protest on their own. O'Connor was a radical, but he also owned land in Ireland and he might be seen as representing an enemy rather than as a supporter of the cause.

When the church bells rang at noon, Charlotte threw her shawl over her shoulders and started toward the Palace to see what was happening. The rain had subsided and a weak sun was breaking through the clouds; the streets were becoming more crowded with barrow men and peddlers. Charlotte stopped for a minute to watch two young girls about nine or ten years old with a tray filled with papers of pins and skeins of thread. "A ha'penny for strong thread; a penny for a pin" they called out as they walked slowly along. Not many people were taking up their invitation, but Charlotte was glad to see a few women stop to buy pins and thread. The girls were dressed in mud-spattered skirts and their feet were bare. They looked chilly in the spring breeze.

As Charlotte got closer to the Palace, the noise of a crowd became louder, and when she walked into the square she saw more than a hundred people gathered in a crowd looking up at the Palace windows.

"We wish to present a petition to the Queen!" their leader shouted. Charlotte recognized Jock, who was at the head of the crowd.

A group of guardsmen were gathering in front of the protesters, their red jackets glittering in the pale sunlight. They held their rifles on their shoulders and the captain stepped forward with a warning:

"Disperse! Disperse all of you! If you do not clear the street, you will be held as traitors to the Queen. Disperse!"

"Has the Queen no heart?" shouted one man. "Will she let her subjects starve at the whim of a cruel landlord?"

"The people of Ireland call on you for justice," called another voice that Charlotte recognized as Walter McGuire's. "We have fought in the Queen's army and worked on her ships. She owes us protection from greedy landlords!"

"Disperse you fools or we shall fire," shouted the captain. He gave a signal to the soldiers behind him who raised their rifles to their shoulders.

Suddenly Charlotte saw a strange sight. A man in a blue turban—Kumar Singh—was walking in front of the guards, looking toward the crowd of protestors. Today he was dressed in the traditional Sikh clothes, not a European suit.

"Peace" Kumar called in a loud calm voice. "The Queen will protect her subjects if you come in peace. We need no more killing for Ireland or for India."

"Get out of our way," shouted the guardsman. Out of the line of fire." Kumar Singh paid no attention but started walking up and down in the space between the two groups.

"Out of the way," shouted one of the demonstrators. "Don't block our view you bloody kaffir!" He stepped toward the Indian and tried to knock him down, but Singh brushed the scrawny youth away as if he were a child. A guardsman standing behind Singh lifted his rifle and swung it at Singh who staggered and almost fell to the ground. But he did not fall; he moved toward the line of demonstrators holding out his arms in an imploring gesture.

Suddenly there was a gunshot and Kumar Singh fell to the ground. The guardsmen moved forward, stepping gingerly over the body of the fallen man. The soldiers in their red jackets looked intimidating, but some of them hesitated as they looked down at the fallen Indian and then at the crowd in front of them. The demonstrators also fell quiet for a moment, and the men in the front line glanced toward one another.

Charlotte felt the pause as if neither side was sure what they should do next.

Then another figure stepped from the sidelines. With a jolt of surprise, Charlotte recognized Captain Granville. He stood in front of the troops and raised his arms. "Forward men! Do not hesitate." Then, facing the mob and waving his walking stick above his head as though it was a sword he cried, "Disperse you fools! How dare you approach the Queen's palace?"

The group of demonstrators was turning into an unruly mob. Some of the men at the back of the crowd started fading away as the fighting grew more intense. "Come on! Don't give up," Charlotte heard Walter McGuire's voice rise above the noise. "We're not going to let anyone stop us from seeing the Queen. We have our rights—move forward. These guards can't stop honest working men."

Suddenly Walter was at the front of the line, waving a gun as he advanced toward the soldiers. A handful of others followed him, but more of the demonstrators were slipping away and disappearing into the small streets and alleys at the side of the plaza. Walter waved his revolver around over his head and then leveled it, aiming at one of the soldiers. Captain Granville moved to protect the guardsman and Walter's shot hit him. Granville fell to the ground not ten feet from where Kumar Singh lay.

Spectators at the sides of the square hovered irresolutely watching. Most were too frightened to move forward, but they didn't quite want to leave either.

And then, abruptly, it was all over. The soldiers regrouped and advanced in a disciplined formation on the demonstrators who melted into a mob of individuals in front of their eyes. The smoke and noise of the guns faded and nothing was left except a small cluster of bewildered-looking demonstrators and on the ground the two bodies—one an Indian with his turban slipping off his head, and the other the tall figure of Captain Granville still clutching his walking stick.

Charlotte saw Walter turn to run away. Most of the other demonstrators were already gone, although Jock was standing close by staring at Walter. He grabbed Walter's arm and tried to drag him away, but the guards soon moved in, broke the two apart and with a few vicious jabs of their rifle butts, forced Jock to the side. Two soldiers grabbed Walter McGuire's arms roughly and led him away while Jock and the few remaining demonstrators watched helplessly.

A squad of soldiers took away the two men who had been shot. Charlotte pushed as close as she dared, trying to see whether either man was still alive. Both of them lay unconscious on the stretchers while the soldiers took them into the Palace yard. Charlotte's stomach churned with fear for them. Why did these demonstrations always lead to bloodshed and death? As she turned to walk home, tears stung her eyes. She remembered how Kumar Singh had helped her get away from the first demonstration she had seen all those weeks ago. He had been kind and helpful. It was hard to believe that anyone would have killed him for trying to keep the peace.

And what of Captain Granville? A few days ago she had been despising him. He had arranged the terrifying kidnapping of Meena and Parni, yet he had escaped punishment because Kumar did not want to pursue the kidnapping charge. And the theft of the emerald was considered part of the spoils of war. Many men had come back from India with treasures in their packs. He had fought for the Queen in India and today he was trying to protect the Queen again. He no more deserved to die than Walter's brother had. Suddenly Charlotte was filled with anger at the Queen and all the aristocrats who watched from safety as young men lost their lives in useless confrontations.

By the time she arrived home, Charlotte wanted to throw herself on the bed and cry. Instead she turned to her Bible and opened it blindly looking for comfort. None of the verses she came upon comforted her. In desperation, she picked up a book of poetry that Daniel had given her

Can I see another's woe,
And not be in sorrow too?
Can I see another's grief,
And not seek for kind relief?

How could the rich and powerful watch the pain their subjects suffered and not be filled with guilt? Walter and Jock had started this demonstration with great hope and faith. They were so certain the Queen would hear the petitioners and respond to their pleas. But no one had bothered to listen to them. Instead the men had been brutally turned back. The soldiers had shot the only peacemaker in their midst because his skin was brown and they feared him. And Walter had shot a man who was trying to do his duty for his country. What good could possibly come of today's events?

CHAPTER TWENTY-SIX

After the Storm

A few minutes later, Daniel came home. Charlotte ran to him and leaned against him as she blurted out the story of the disastrous demonstration.

"I can scarcely believe such terrible things could happen just because of a street demonstration," Charlotte said. "We had better go to the Singh house and find out whether Meena has heard about what has happened."

When Rahil opened the door for them, they enquired about Kumar Singh and were told only that he was not at home. Everything was quiet and peaceful, so obviously the news had not arrived. Charlotte decided she would visit Meena Kaur while Daniel told Rahil the news and gave him the practical details of what had happened.

Charlotte entered the by-now familiar parlor to find Meena sitting at her small desk writing a letter. She jumped up to greet Charlotte and clapped her hands for Parni to come and fetch some tea.

"Why are you looking so grave, my friend?" asked Meena. "Is it not a beautiful spring day when the rain has forgotten to fall even in London?"

"I have very bad news," Charlotte could barely get the words out in the face of Meena's cheerful approach. "Earlier this afternoon I went to the Chartist demonstration in front of Buckingham Palace. Your husband was there too. I saw him across the square."

"Yes, he told me he thought he would go to watch the demonstration. He believes the Queen will at last pay attention to her poorer subjects and will offer them some relief. Did the Queen appear, or did she send a minister to listen to the petition?"

"I am afraid she did neither. Instead, the guards stood with their guns pointed at the demonstrators and ordered them to leave. No one would take their petition. No official appeared from the Palace to listen to their grievances. Some of the men became very angry and demanded that the Queen or Prince Albert pay attention to them. They advanced upon the guards and the situation grew tense.

"Just then I saw your husband walk into the gap between the soldiers and the demonstrators. He tried to calm the crowd. To persuade them to remain peaceful. Oh, I don't know how to tell you this! A terrible thing happened." Charlotte paused and led Meena to a comfortable chair.

"The soldiers were angry with your husband. Angry even though he was just telling everyone that they should be peaceful. I heard a shot fired and your husband fell to the ground."

Meena shuddered and jumped from the chair. "Oh, no! That cannot have happened! Why would they shoot at someone who was trying to preserve peace? My husband is a good man and a mighty warrior. He would not allow himself to be frightened or brought down by a line of guards even if they carried guns. He was not fighting the soldiers." Meena twisted the edge of her tunic. Parni stepped close to her and put her hand comfortingly on her mistress's arm.

"I am very much afraid that is what happened. Difficult though it is to believe. A few minutes after your husband fell, something else terrible happened. Captain Granville was shot by someone in the crowd of protesters. The demonstration ended quickly after that and both your husband and Captain Granville were taken away by the soldiers. I believe they have been taken to the Army hospital."

Meena Singh sank into the chair by the fireplace. Charlotte perched on the arm of the chair and encircled Meena with her arm as the woman began to sob. "How shall I live without my husband to guide me?" wailed Meena. "I have sworn to love and serve him all the days of my life. How can he be taken from me so swiftly and so cruelly?"

"We do not know for certain that he has been killed," Charlotte reassured her. "We must find out where he is and how he is being cared for."

Charlotte left Parni to the task of consoling Meena, while she went to fetch Daniel and see what he and Rahil had discussed. Soon they were all together in the parlor. Meena was bravely composing herself and stifling her tears. "I must go to my husband. I must find out how severe his wounds are," she said. "I will take care of him and get him the best medical care available. He is strong. I will make sure he recovers his health and strength. And I shall find a way to take revenge on the person who dared to shoot him. No man who has done that deserves to live."

Charlotte was surprised to see how quickly Meena assumed the responsibility of handling the household while her husband was injured and needed her care. She started giving directions to Rahil.

"You, Rahil, will take a message to the men who have worked with my husband. You know the houses my husband has visited in his efforts to establish relations with the Queen. Perhaps I will talk to some of them..." Her voice trailed off and then she continued speaking to Rahil in Punjabi as she gave more directions.

Daniel volunteered to go to the Army barracks and ask about Kumar Singh's condition and find out where he had been taken. Charlotte shuddered as she wondered whether Daniel would learn that their friend was injured or whether he would discover that the bullet had killed him. The torment of waiting was difficult to bear.

Meanwhile Charlotte went down to the kitchen to let the cook and the kitchen maid know of the terrible accident that had befallen the family. For the first time the cook seemed sympathetic. "That poor young Mrs. Singh!" she exclaimed. "What a shock this must be for her. Don't you worry, Molly and me will take care to see that the house keeps running."

Charlotte knew the experienced cook would be able to organize the kitchen and make sure everyone in the household was fed and that guests who called to offer sympathy would be taken care of.

As the day wore on, and Daniel had not returned, Charlotte decided she had better go back to her own house. Meena instructed Rahil to escort her there through the dark streets and they all gathered their patience to wait for more news about Kumar Singh and his fate. The day that had started off with high hopes had become a complete disaster.

The next day passed in a flurry of activity. Daniel was able to locate Kumar Singh in the Army treatment center. He had not been killed by the shot, but he had been gravely injured. When Meena Kaur was able to see her husband, an Army surgeon told her the bullet should be removed as soon as possible. Otherwise infection would set in and her husband would almost certainly die.

That evening, the surgery took place, with an Army sergeant holding a lamp while the surgeon cut into the flesh of Kumar Singh's chest to find the bullet. Kumar

Singh asked the doctor to put a cloth in his mouth so he could bite into it when the pain became too intense. With that meager help he was able to remain stoic, as Sikh warriors were trained to do, and to get through the surgery without betraying any sign of the pain he was enduring. After probing the wound, the doctor was able to locate the bullet and remove it.

When the surgeon met Meena Kaur afterward, he told her that her husband had a good chance of surviving his surgery as long as infection could be kept out of the wound. He added, "I have never seen a man who endured so much pain without showing any sign of weakness or fear".

The sergeant who had held the lamp added, "I never figured a brown-skinned savage could put up with so much suffering without a whimper. No wonder they fought our troops to a standstill in the Punjab."

During the week after the demonstration, several newspapers wrote stories about the events and the two men who had been shot. But as Kumar Singh slowly recovered, the public ceased paying attention to his actions on the day of the protest. Because he had survived the attack, the police were reluctant to spend time on the crime and few people in the city were concerned about the wounding of an unknown man from a faraway alien heathen country.

Captain Granville was not as lucky as Kumar Singh. When a surgeon tried to remove the bullet from Granville's chest, he found it was lodged very close to the heart. Hugh Granville had lost a great deal of blood from the wound and when the doctor tried to remove the bullet, the Captain died.

The attention of the press and public then focused on the man who had killed Captain Granville—Walter McGuire. He had been taken into custody immediately after the shooting. His guilt was obvious to everyone because his actions had been seen by several people. When the soldiers seized him, he was still carrying the gun he had used to shoot Captain Granville. He was sent to the notorious Newgate Prison to await a trial, although, as the newspapers pointed out, no one doubted what the verdict would be.

When it came time for his trial, Walter faced a judge with a reputation for giving harsh sentences for almost any violent crime. Lord Dunwoody had been born into one of the wealthiest families in the country. His family owned, it was said, half of the land in Lincolnshire. His father could ride for three days and never leave land that was part of his estate. The only poverty Lord Dunwoody had seen in his life was the rural poverty of tenants who had trouble surviving an especially hard winter or a series of dry summers. As a generous but firm landlord, he had extended time for the payment of rents when a tenant was hit by unexpected disaster, but he expected a full day's work from every tenant and insisted that those who would not work must leave his estate.

When Lord Dunwoody came to London to sit in the House of Lords, he discovered a city such as he had never seen or dreamed of. During his early days in the city, he had often taken one of his favorite horses and ridden around the city as he had been used to doing on his estates. He saw the hundreds of ragged children walking the streets selling treats or toys and he shuddered at the wasted lives. Within the House of Lords he frequently called upon his fellow peers to give justice on their lands so their tenants could make a reasonable living. When the Chartists started calling for votes for every man, he struggled to believe that uneducated working men could be trusted to make decisions for the country. He was afraid the Chartists would start a revolution like the ones in America and France fifty years earlier. Now he was called upon to judge an undoubted crime that had been committed by a Chartist supporter. He knew that he had sworn to uphold the law and he was prepared to take whatever measures were necessary to ensure that justice was done.

CHAPTER TWENTY-SEVEN

Trial of a Radical

The trial started on April 7 at the courthouse known as
Old Bailey, which was adjacent to the Newgate Prison.
Daniel had an appointment to meet with a member of
Parliament, but Charlotte was determined to see the
trial no matter how grim the occasion, and Kathleen
declared she would like to see it too. It was a gray day
with dark layers of clouds making the morning look
like twilight as they walked toward the grim bulk of
Old Bailey and filed in with the other curious
onlookers. Even though the visitors' gallery was
crowded, they managed to get seats that gave them a
view of the judge, the jury, and the prisoner's box. As
they took their seats, the courtroom looked dark and
gloomy but soon the court clerks lit the brass
chandeliers and by the time Lord Dunwoody entered,
the room looked bright and almost cheerful.

Walter McGuire was led into the courtroom by two
guards. His shirt and corduroy trousers were sweat-
stained and shabby and his face was pale and drawn.
His hair was unkempt and he scowled as his eyes swept

around the spectator benches looking for a friendly face. When he saw Charlotte and Kathleen, his lips twisted into a slight smile, but his eyes kept searching for other familiar figures.

"Oh, he is so thin! They must be treating him cruelly," Kathleen whispered to Charlotte, who nodded in agreement.

Justice Lord Dunwoody, in his elaborately curled white wig, sat upright on the judge's bench with his clerk beside him holding a sheaf of papers. The jury of twelve land-owning men were in their box watching and listening as the prosecuting lawyer described the crime. He told the jury how the demonstrators had marched toward the soldiers who were on duty protecting Buckingham Palace. He called upon three witnesses who swore they had been at the demonstration and had seen the defendant, Walter McGuire, raise his gun and fire at the line of soldiers and shoot, hitting the victim, Hugh Granville, who had been standing in front of the soldiers.

"After great suffering and pain," the prosecutor intoned, "Captain Granville died while a surgeon was attempting to remove the fatal bullet. Walter McGuire is guilty of murder and the Crown asks that he be sentenced to death by hanging for his crime."

Judge Dunwoody looked sternly at the prisoner and then around the courtroom. "Is there anyone present who wishes to speak for this defendant?"

Charlotte realized that the moment she was dreading had arrived. Her knees trembled, but she stood up straight and spoke directly to the judge: "Your Lordship, I would like to say a few words about the man who was unfortunately killed. I believe there is information which explains that this defendant was not the only guilty person in this case."

"Young lady, are you the prisoner's wife or his sister?" Lord Dunwoody peered at Charlotte as he spoke.

"Neither, your honor. My husband and I are friends of Walter McGuire and we wish to be sure that all the information is put before the court."

"I have never had a woman address my court, and I cannot accept the testimony of a married woman. Your husband has the duty to speak for you. This is a man's business. Please sit down."

There was nothing Charlotte could do except sink back into her seat. She knew that the crimes Captain Granville had committed could not excuse Walter's action, but she had hoped the judge would be more merciful if he knew the background of the case. Captain Granville had tried to lead the radicals into committing criminal acts in order to discredit their cause. He had supplied the gun to Walter and had enticed him into kidnapping Meena. The cycle of violence he had started had finally led to his death.

While Charlotte sat in a daze of disappointment, she heard a buzz at the back of the gallery of spectators.

"Make way for Lord Granville," boomed a loud voice, as a tall, thin man in carefully tailored black clothes made his way toward the front of the court. He walked slowly, leaning on a stick while holding onto the arm of a servant. In a frail voice he spoke directly to the judge. "I am Lord Alfred Granville, brother of the deceased Captain Granville. I would like to address the court."

Room was quickly made for Lord Granville and the judge, lawyers and jurymen all watched him closely as he spoke in a weak but clear voice.

"As you know, my only brother Captain Hugh Granville, served Queen and country as an Army officer for many years. He served in India and before that in Her Majesty's colony in Jamaica. While he was away from home for a number of years, our mother died and our father spent most of his time in London. He incurred a number of debts that put the future of our estates in danger. Both my brother and I have been struggling to keep our property intact and pay off our father's debts.

"Although my brother and I worked for the same goal, I have noticed a change in him since he returned from his service in India. He became obsessed with the idea that England was slipping into the hands of foreigners and a rabble who would not preserve our country. Recently, through his letters and through conversations I had with him, I discovered that he was responsible for several crimes. As you can see, I am a sick man. I am in fact a dying man and as a matter of honor I want to acknowledge the crimes of our family

"My brother was responsible for the theft of a precious jewel while he was in India, but I will not dwell on that because the jewel has been returned to its owner. But as we all know, one crime leads to another. My brother was also responsible for the death of a young servant in a fire that he started deliberately to frighten off a man, a foreigner, who had come to our city. And he was responsible for arranging the kidnapping of two innocent women as well as for providing some radical young men with guns in the hope that they would be incited to commit violent acts. He thought these radicals would be caught and severely punished. My brother believed he was preserving the honor of our family. Our family has served this country well for many centuries. Unfortunately, my brother's attempts to preserve the values of the old England led to injustice and crimes that he was too blind to acknowledge."

Lord Granville's voice sank to a whisper and he started to cough. His servant stepped forward to hand him a handkerchief, but he waved the man away.

"I must finish what I have to say before my death ends our family forever. None of my brother's crimes justify his murder, but I felt impelled to lay them before the court. Perhaps knowing the provocation caused by my brother's foolish and wicked actions, the jury may think differently about the crime committed by Walter

McGuire. I fear that the poor and landless people of our country have suffered much during these difficult years."

Lord Granville's voice sank to a low murmur and dissolved into a fit of coughing as his servant led him away from the judge's bench and back to his seat. For several moments there was complete silence in the court. Then Justice Lord Dunwoody looked at the Walter McGuire, who was sitting in the prisoner's dock looming high above the courtroom. "Lord Granville has given us valuable information about the victim in this crime, however, Captain Granville's faults are not germane to the case before us. This is a trial for his murder. Has the accused prisoner anything to say?"

"Yes, your Honor, I would like to explain something of what caused this tragedy. As Lord Granville has graciously said, many people in this country have suffered much because of the greed of those who are called our betters. The Queen is the protector of all the people who live in her realm. My friends and I marched to Buckingham Palace that fateful day to present a petition to the Queen. We sincerely believed that Her Majesty would not countenance the cruelty being visited upon her subjects if she heard their accounts of the state of the people in her realm.

"You may have heard of the tragedy at Ballinglass in Ireland, where, at the whim of a landlord, families were driven from the homes they had occupied for years. Not only were they evicted from their homes, they were driven out of the village and not allowed to accept the charity of neighbors. All of the tenants in the village were ordered not to give shelter or food to those who had lost their homes. This is not the way landlords in a great country like Britain are supposed to behave. The time is coming when the Queen and all the lords of the realm will understand what has been happening. I take the liberty of giving you the words of the Chartist anthem:

We men of bone of shrunken shank,
Our only treasure dearth,
Women who carry at their breast
Heirs to the hungry earth,
Heirs to the hungry earth

Speak with one voice, we march we rest,
And march again upon the years
Sons of our sons are listening,
To hear the Chartist cheers
Oh, to hear the Chartists cheers.

As Walter spoke, Charlotte looked around the courtroom and noticed that some members of the jury shifted in their seats as they listened. Some glared at Walter, others looked curious and two of them actually smiled. Lord Dunwoody was leaning forward listening intently. After giving his statement in a firm, strong voice, Walter sat down. The judge leaned back in his seat and clasped his hands together. For several seconds he was silent, saying nothing to the jury or the court. Finally he straightened up and announced:

"The jury may now deliberate. The Court will be adjourned until two o'clock. At that time we will reconvene and I will announce the jury's decision and will impose the appropriate sentence."

Spectators and jurymen rose and shuffled out of the room. There was a buzz of conversation. "Most unusual," Charlotte heard one red-faced, white-haired man mutter disapprovingly. Other spectators who had been expecting to hear the judge quickly condemn a man to hang looked disappointed. An air of tension filled the room.

When the trial reconvened, the foreman of the jury announced the verdict they had reached after a short deliberation: Walter McGuire was guilty of murder and the jury recommended he be sentenced to be hanged. Lord Dunwoody frowned and listened gravely but did not immediately pronounce his decision about the sentence. Instead he made a brief speech:

"The jury has reached its verdict. Walter McGuire is guilty of shooting Captain Granville and wounding him so grievously that he died. At the same time, the Court recognizes that the man who died had committed terrible acts that caused great harm to several British subjects and aroused great passion in many working men some of whom have been harshly treated by landowners and employers. The Lord sometimes works in mysterious ways to bring about justice and this court seeks to promote justice throughout the Queen's realm. The Court acknowledges the right of the demonstrators to bring a petition before the Queen. Unfortunately the guards at Buckingham Palace did not respect this right, which led to disorder and eventually the killing. Any man who shoots and kills another must atone for this crime, but when the death is the result of an honest attempt to uphold the rights of British subjects, the man should be given an opportunity to repent and mend his life before going to meet his Maker. I therefore sentence Walter McGuire to transportation to a penal colony in distant Australia where he can redeem his life through repentance, prayer, and good works."

The dramatic end to such a high-profile crime set off a flurry of gossip throughout the courtroom and across the city. Walter McGuire was taken back to Newgate Prison where he would remain until a suitable ship to transport him and other prisoners on the long journey to Australia was ready to sail.

CHAPTER TWENTY-EIGHT

Farewell to the Old World

The trial of Walter McGuire was the biggest news story of the season and Daniel was kept busy preparing articles and interviewing people involved. Charlotte admired the way he presented the case for the demonstrators:

A massive demonstration held outside Buckingham Palace on Sunday afternoon became violent when the Palace Guards tried to force the demonstrators to disband and go home. The confrontation led to the reckless use of guns and left two injured men lying on the pavement after the soldiers had finally driven the demonstrators away. One man, Kumar Singh, a Sikh from India and a stranger to this city, was struck by a bullet while he tried to preserve peace between the two groups. He was seriously wounded, but is slowly recovering from his wounds. Doctors are hopeful that he will survive the attack. The other man, Captain Hugh Granville, who had served his country in India for several years, died of his wound. Has England become a country where this kind of violence is used routinely to prevent communication between the poor and the government?

Many people questioned whether justice had been administered. The speech Walter had made in court was transcribed and distributed as a broadsheet throughout the country. The dramatic trial and especially the unexpected decision by Lord Dunwoody to sentence Walter to transportation rather than hanging were topics discussed frequently in pubs and coffee houses.

While the authorities waited for an available ship to take him and other prisoners to Australia, Walter remained in prison. Newgate Prison, an ugly hulk of a building, was built around a central indoor courtyard designed to allow the guards to keep watch on all of the prisoners in the surrounding cells. Each small dark cell held eight or ten prisoners and was furnished with nothing but straw thrown on the floor for bedding and buckets for sanitation. With no outside windows, prisoners had to grope around the cells by the dim light from the central court.

Food rations were scanty and often rancid but friends could provide more food by bribing one of the guards with coins or a drink. Tom and Jock and a couple of the other dock workers saw to it that Walter got extra food. Jock was far more subdued than he had been when he visited the Gallaghers and talked so hopefully of the future. His faith in the Chartist movement had dimmed after he had seen the devastating effects on Walter's life.

"If I hadn't talked Walter into taking that gun, this would never have happened," he confided to Daniel one afternoon as they were leaving the prison. "All the men I talked into joining the Chartists are worried now. You never met Jude—he was the man who pretended to be the sexton. He thought it was a lark, but after Granville was captured, he was scared. He took to his heels and ran off back to Cornwall where he came from. We'll never see him again. And now we'll probably never see Walter again. I thought we could change things and make them better, but nothing has changed."

Kathleen visited Walter in prison as often as she could. She had been very impressed by his eloquent speech at the trial, and she was charmed by the bravery with which he faced the future. He told her his plans for starting a new life after he had served his sentence. He began to encourage her to think about following him to Australia to make a new start in life. She redoubled her efforts in Charlotte's classes, bending over her slate and copying maxims that she thought would help her grow up quickly. She and Walter talked of taking up farming in Australia and raising a family far away from the poverty of both Ireland and England.

Meena Kaur and Charlotte grew closer as they tried to help Kumar Singh regain his strength and health. Like Walter, Kumar was disillusioned with the British government. His emerald had been found and he was pleased to be able to return that treasure to his native Punjab. But his efforts to speak to British leaders had led to nothing. He had expected to be treated respectfully as a representative of his people. Instead he had been scorned as the member of an alien race and treated as an inferior. He determined to return to his people and continue the struggle to keep them free from British rule.

"My husband is unhappy with the results of our visit to England," Meena told Charlotte. "When I came to England, I thought it was a grand place where everyone was rich and happy. Instead, I have found that most people are poor, almost as poor as the peasants in the Punjab. I will be happy to go back to my own country where I have many friends and relatives. Perhaps when I return there, I will become a teacher like you and teach our servants and the peasants who work the land to read. People need knowledge before they can become free."

"You may find your country changed from when you left," Charlotte reminded her. "You have been here more than two years now. When I returned to England after twelve years in America, I found it a different country from the one I remembered. Or perhaps I looked on it with different eyes. My brother grew up while I was away and I am very glad to know him and his wife as adults now. That is one good thing. But nothing here is as I remember it. Most of all I have changed. I want a different life from any I could have imagined while I was growing up in England."

"Yes, I have changed too. I have grown up," agreed Meena. "I am no longer a young bride as I was when I left my home. I know now that I am not a child, but a strong woman. I believe that I will be able to help my husband and my people." She blushed and leaned toward Charlotte to whisper, "I hope to give my husband a son in a few months. Then I will be a mother and a responsible adult. I have learned a great deal in England. And I will never forget the friends I made."

Charlotte shared a confidence with her, "I hope to have another child this winter too. This time perhaps all will go well. Having a child will change both of our lives. I will write to you and let you know what happens. Perhaps the next time we meet we will both be the mothers of families."

Another month went by before the ship bound for Botany Bay was prepared to sail. It was ready to lift anchor on the morning tide, and Charlotte and Daniel as well as Kathleen walked toward the dock to see whether they could get a glimpse of Walter before he left. The sun was starting to rise as they walked through the early-morning streets, quiet except for the rumble of farm wagons bringing produce to the markets. Charlotte was startled to see a group of young women walking in single file down the street with baskets of ripe strawberries on their heads. They were tall, sunburned country girls in dark dresses walking with measured steps and singing softly as they carefully balanced the heavy baskets of berries.

"That's good luck," Kathleen murmured. "Everyone says it's good luck to see the strawberry girls. It means that spring has come to stay and we've lived through another hard winter. Oh, I hope it will be good luck for Walter on his dangerous long journey."

As they neared the docks, they could see the convict ship bobbing up and down in the river current. "It's a terrible small ship for such a long voyage," Kathleen complained.

"Maybe they don't have a great number of convicts for this trip," Charlotte reassured her, although the ship looked frighteningly small to her too. "It has three masts and is a two decker. It will be a safe ship. And look—her name is *Lady Margaret*—such a gentle name for a ship."

Soon they were joined by Jock, who wanted to catch a last glimpse of his friend.

"This is a sad day for all of us," he said. "But we won't give up hope. Walter will start again in Australia. And as for me, I'm going back home to work with the Chartists there. It may take a long time, but we'll make old England change before we die."

"Here come the prisoners," Daniel pointed to the line of convicts, bound together with chains, climbing down from the open wagon in which they had been brought from the prison.

The men walked slowly toward the ship, sometimes stumbling as they dragged the heavy chains that linked their feet together. Guards walking alongside them watched them carefully and urged them on by hitting them with long wooden staffs. A few spectators jeered at them, while family members crowded alongside the dock to watch. Occasionally a woman would call out a greeting, but if a prisoner answered, he was given a swift crack of the guard's rod.

When the four of them saw Walter in the line, looking as pale and bedraggled as the rest of them, but holding his head high and trying to pick out familiar faces in the crowd, they waved eagerly.

"Oh, Walter, Walter, you'll not forget me, will you?" Kathleen cried out. "I'll pray for you every day."

Walter smiled bravely and tossed his head toward her until a cuff from one of the guards forced him to look down at the ground again. But as he walked past them, they could hear his familiar voice singing softly, "Men of England..." and soon other prisoners defiantly joined in. As they walked up the gangplank to the ship, the strains of the hymn rang out clearly.

Men of England, wherefore plough
For the lords who lay ye low?
Wherefore weave with toil and care
The rich robes your tyrants wear?

"Despite everything, Walter will be all right. If he keeps up that spirit," Daniel whispered into Charlotte's ear. "I've no doubt he will soon be mounting demonstrations in Australia just as he and his friends have in London. Maybe they will turn Australia into another America."

"There would be nothing wrong with that, Daniel Gallagher, and you will no doubt be writing the book that will inspire them to do it."

Afterword: Historical Figures and Events

Queen Victoria (1819-1901) The Queen's guards had good reason to believe that the Queen might be in danger from crowds and demonstrators. Soon after she assumed the throne in 1837, as she was riding in a carriage with her husband, she was shot at by a man who suddenly appeared out of the crowd and rushed toward her. By 1846, the year this novel is set, there had been four attempts on her life, most of them by men who were later judged to be insane. During all of her long reign, seven attempts made to assassinate her. Although some of the assailants were found guilty of the crime and sentenced to death, none of these sentences were carried out. Instead they were transmuted to transportation to Australian penal colonies.

Feargus O'Connor (1794-1855) Born into an aristocratic Protestant family in County Cork, O'Connor became a champion of political reform and of the Chartist principles of a vote for every man. In 1832, he was elected as a Member of Parliament where he spoke principally to support Irish causes. He was a charismatic speaker and was featured at many public meetings. He also founded

279

a radical newspaper *Northern Star*. As he grew older, he became increasingly eccentric and quarreled with many of his colleagues in Parliament, sometimes violently. In 1852 he was confined to an asylum for the insane. More than 40,000 people attended his funeral procession when he died in 1855.

Margaret Fuller (1810-1850) Born in Massachusetts, Margaret Fuller was one of the most influential American writers and journalists of the early nineteenth century. She was a friend and associate of Ralph Waldo Emerson, Henry Thoreau and others of their circle. Her most famous book, *Women in the Nineteenth Century*, influenced later feminists including Elizabeth Cady Stanton and Susan B. Anthony. During the 1840s she traveled in the United States and Europe as a journalist for Horace Greeley's newspaper the *Tribune*. Margaret Fuller makes a cameo appearance in each of the Charlotte Edgerton mystery series.

George W. M. Reynolds (1814-1879) During his lifetime, the stories written by George W. M. Reynolds were more popular than those of either Dickens or Thackeray. He wrote gothic stories of werewolves and vampires and was most famous for his book *The Mysteries of London*. Besides writing fiction, Reynolds was a radical journalist who believed in the Chartists' principles. To further this cause, he started two radical newspapers. When Chartism dwindled after the 1850s, he continued his work as a journalist and became a supporter of republicanism in England.

British Museum. The British Museum was first opened to the public in 1759, almost 100 years before this book takes place. It was a new kind of museum, founded by private citizens who wished to share their collections of objects and books with the public. The objects that formed the basis of its first collection came from Sir Hans Sloane, an 18th century doctor, who collected historical and scientific specimens as a hobby. The Museum's collections grew as the British empire expanded and artifacts from Egypt, Greece and the Middle East were added. In 1840, the Museum sent its first expedition overseas to excavate antiquities to be added to the collection. Today the Museum has grown to contain over 13 million object and the largest online database of objects of any museum in the world.

George Scharf (1820-1895) Raised by his artist father to be a commercial portrait painter, George Scharf was invited to accompany Charles Fellowes's expedition to Asia Minor for the British Museum. During the trip Scharf drew pictures of the ancient buildings in Xanthos and Lycia. He returned to England with a number of paintings as well as art objects to add to the Museum's collections. Later in life he was a critic and lecturer and eventually became the director of the new National Portrait Gallery.

Ballinglass The failure of the potato crop in Ireland in 1845 brought distress to many farmers in Ireland because potatoes were their staple and often their only crop. Without crops to sell, tenants could not pay their rents and could be evicted from their farms. The British government made some attempt to help the Irish by shipping corn to Ireland, but the relief was not nearly enough to hold off starvation, evictions, and emigration. The sensation caused by the evictions in Ballinglass, Galway, was that the tenants involved were relatively prosperous. They were not behind in their rents and they had even improved the land they lived on by clearing a 400-acre bog. Their landlord, Mrs. Gerrard, decided she wanted to use her land for cattle grazing because it was more profitable than farming, so she called on the sheriff, police, and the British Army to evict 300 tenants from her land on March 13, 1846. Their houses were demolished and neighbors were forbidden to give them shelter. The scandal was so great that the event was investigated by Lord

Londonberry of Ulster, who spoke in the House of Lords to say he was "deeply grieved" by what happened. But the decision was not changed and the tenants were left without their land and homes.

Chartism During the first half of the 19th century, British society was going through a series of changes that made life difficult for many workers. Farm workers were being driven from their traditional life because of the invention of machinery to help with planting, cultivating and harvesting crops. People who made their living by spinning, weaving and other handicrafts were losing jobs because machines could now do their work much cheaper and faster than any human being could. One solution proposed to make life in England more equal was to change the politics of the country. The Charter would give every man a vote, provide secret ballots, enable people who were not landowners to serve in Parliament, provide a salary for members of Parliament, have an election every year, and equalize the population of all Parliamentary constituencies. Thousands of people supported the idea of adopting the Charter during the 1840s; however, the movement gradually declined after 1850. Most of the reforms advocated by Chartists were eventually adopted.

East India Company In 1600, Queen Elizabeth I gave a charter to the East India Company to establish trading with foreign countries. Wealthy merchants and aristocrats owned stock in the company, which gradually dominated trade between Great Britain and India. After 1757, the Company became the de facto ruler of India, a position it held for a century. The Company ruled India through its private army and with the cooperation of British government forces. After the Indian rebellion of 1858, the British government took over direct control of India.

Sikhism About 500 years ago the Sikh religion developed in the Punjab region of India. It has grown to be the smallest of the world's major religions; about 27 million people in the world identify themselves as Sikhs. The majority of Sikhs still live in the Punjab although there are large colonies in other parts of India and in Europe and North America. Sikhs believe in one God and in the equality of all people. They reject religious rituals such as fasting, pilgrimages, and animal sacrifice, as well as the Hindu caste system. Their religious leaders are called gurus.

Sikh Wars During Queen Victoria's reign, the British conducted a series of small wars most of which involved England's colonial ambitions. At the beginning of the 19th century, India was made up of a number of small kingdoms some of which submitted peacefully to British trade and domination, while others resisted strongly. Ranjit Singh, founder of the Sikh empire in the Punjab, fought against British incursions, but after he died in 1839, his heirs fought with one another for control of his empire. The first Sikh War occurred in 1845-46 and the second one from1848-49. Both the Sikh warriors and the British Army fought bravely, but there were sharp cultural differences in the way they waged wars. Many fighters on both sides believed their enemies were fighting unfairly and many developed lifelong resentments.

Khanda The major symbol of the Sikh religion is the khanda, a circular form in which the central line is a two-edged sword with its blade surrounded by a circle made of two curved single-edged swords. The hilt of the central sword, pointing downward, is intersected by the crossing hilts of the two single-edged swords.

Sources of Quotations in the Text

Chapter 4. p.26. "Ye working men of Britain…" A broadsheet printed in 1838. From *The Chartists: Popular Politics in the Industrial Revolution* by Dorothy Thompson (Pantheon 1984)

Chapter 8. pp. 70 and 72. Traditional nursery rhymes. p. 71 "Little Lamb" by William Blake.

Chapter 9. p.78. "The Mountains of Mourne" by Perry French

Chapter 10. p. 94. "Barbara Allen" a popular folk song that exists in many versions.

Chapter 11. p. 110. "Chartist Song" by Thomas Cooper from *The Anthology of Leicester Chartist Song. Poetry & Verse* edited by Ned Newitt, (Leicester Pioneer Press 2006)

Chapter 12. p. 117. "Ho! The car Emancipation…" *Singing for Freedom: The Hutchinson Family Singers and the Nineteenth-Century Culture of Reform* (Yale Univ. Pr. 2007)

Chapter 13. p. 123. "Men of England" by Percy Bysshe Shelley

Chapter 14. p. 134."Rule Britannia" by James Thompson 1740; pp. 134-5. "Yankee Doodle" Popular song of the American Revolution; often attributed to Dr. Richard Shuckburgh

Chapter 17. p. 159. "Men of England" by Percy Bysshe Shelley

Chapter 18. p. 163. "What ails thee, Lucy Wan?" British folk song collected in Child's *English and Scottish Ballads*; p. 170. "Sad the bird.." an old Irish lament translated by Charlotte Brooke in *Reliques of Irish Poetry* (1789)

Chapter 22. p. 202. "Chartist Anthem" by Ben Boucher 1847; p. 208. traditional nursery rhyme "Paddy was a Welshman..." .

Chapter 23. p. 215. "Chartist Song" by Thomas Cooper from *The Anthology of Leicester Chartist Song, Poetry & Verse* edited by Ned Newitt, (Leicester Pioneer Press 2006)

Chapter 25, p. 233. "Bold Fenian Men" Irish rebel ballad by Kearney Peadar; p. 240. "On Another's Sorrow" by William Blake.

Chapter 27, p. 257. "Chartist Anthem" by Ben Boucher 1847.

Chapter 28, p. 267. "Men of England" by Percy Bysshe Shelley

www.ingramcontent.com/pod-product-compliance
Lightning Source LLC
Chambersburg PA
CBHW051415170626
46809CB00006B/2169